AF442805

CONTENTS

A CAMCORDER VIDEO CAPTURES THE SETTING OF THE STORY, AN ANTIQUE PADDLE WHEELER BOAT ON THE MOVE - THREE TIERS OF WHITE EDWARDIAN CONFECTION WITH SIDE WHEELER PADDLES CHURNING THE WATER.

S.S. 'BELLE EPOQUE': A LUXURY NILE STEAM VESSEL FROM A GLORIOUS ERA.

VOICE OVER (Daniel Cane, cruise Egyptologist): "As the paddle wheels of the *Belle Epoque* slowly turn like the pages of a vintage Agatha Christie detective novel, a contemporary 'mock murder' mystery game was supposed to commence aboard the luxury Nile cruise boat.

But all is not as it seems...

CHAPTER 1
Feather of Truth

Daniel stuck out his tongue in the cabin's gilded vanity mirror.

It was the first morning on the River Nile after leaving Cairo.

The guest Egyptologist had slept in and was brushing his teeth in the cabin's marble and brass bathroom aboard *S.S. Belle Epoque,* when he'd spotted something odd.

But it wasn't the rudeness of his poked out tongue in the reflection that made him pull back as if offended.

It was a mark on his tongue. A blemish on the surface. He blinked blearily at his reflection. Coffee stain? No, not a stain, he decided, diving close to the mirror again. An image. *A green feather shape.* Painted on the surface of his tongue in outline.

A feather?

"Wha- tha- hell?" he said around his protruding tongue, like a victim of strangulation, his eyes splashes of wonderment.

He wiggled the tongue. The feather shape danced.

Some unknown Nile contagion? Maybe fur on his tongue from drinking period-style gin slings with his girlfriend Kate the night before?

No, a distinct feather shape, drawn in what looked like green ink.

He spat out. He gargled with water. He brushed again.

Rotating-oscillating bristles on the head of his electric toothbrush tickled the buds of his tongue, but failed to remove the blemish.

Then he recalled that in ancient Egypt the symbol of a tall ostrich plume represented the goddess of Truth, Balance and Justice, Maat. Priests of the Goddess of Truth, drew an image of her feather on their tongues with green dye so that the words they spoke would be the truth and now a dream of the night before came back to him. The Lady of Truth appeared to him in this dream, blindingly beautiful as truth itself, a tall ostrich feather stuck in her headband. She spoke.

"Daniel, open your mouth."

It was a command that he had no difficulty in obeying. He was already gaping in surprise at her transcendent irruption into his life. Now she leaned forward with a writing instrument in her fingers, a scribal pen in the form of a pointed reed, which she scribbled over his tongue.

Aargh.

The tickling produced the gag reflex; it was that true to life.

But dreams were dreams and mythology was mythology.

This view in the mirror was real. A feather, the hieroglyph for truth sat on his tongue. Unless he was still dreaming, or mythology had broken into his life.

It triggered a memory of another incident, flashing into his mind like light on the mirror from a porthole.

On the day before, he'd been approached by a hawker, while strolling with Kate in the narrow, cobbled streets of *Khan el Kalili* Bazaar in Cairo, a sprawling, glowing Aladdin's Cave of tourist treasures.

Kate had dived into a perfumery stall when a hawker stepped out and dangled a trinket before Daniel's eyes

"Genuine, Sir," said. He was an old man wearing a threadbare *galabea* and a grin.

Daniel immediately recognised the object in his fingers - an amulet of the goddess Maat in green faience. It depicted her neatly squatting, a long skirt stretched over her knees. A single ostrich feather protruded from her headband, her divine symbol. The 'feather of truth.' Used in the underworld scales of justice to weigh the guilt or innocence of a dead person's heart and decide their worthiness to enter heaven.

"Not today, thanks," Daniel said.

Buying 'antiquities' from locals, even obvious fakes made for the tourist trade, was not something Egyptologists ought to do, even glorified tour guides like Daniel Cane.

He moved on a little further, eyeing a stall with exotic bottles in multi-coloured blown glass, like miniature minarets. They looked like perfume bottles, which made him wonder how Kate was going at the Egyptian perfumery stall.

He turned his head and found the old man still there, dangling the amulet.

"Special for you, Sir."

Daniel was about to shake his head again when he detected a certain appeal in the Egyptian's eye. Chronic low tourism levels, exacerbated by a pandemic, had devastated the local population as much as low River Nile levels once did in ancient times.

The trinket was a pretty fake, he thought, taking it from him to look at.

Daniel eventually succumbed to the old man's grin and bought the Maat amulet.

Against professional instincts.

"What have you got?" Kate said, appearing with a small wrapped purchase in her hand.

"A little amulet keepsake," he said. "Maat, Goddess of truth and justice. See, she has the ostrich feather of truth on her head. Her priests used to paint a green feather on their tongues so that they would always speak and judge the truth, weighing innocence and guilt in fairness. And you, Kate? Did you find a perfume?"

"I bought this lovely fragrance for the cruise. Feathery and mysterious. Goes by the promising name of Fragrant Nefertiti. Do you like it?" She leaned forward, offering her cheek and ear.

Daniel breathed in the fragrance of Kate.

"You smell wonderful."

"And you're a big liar. Just a test. I actually haven't put any on. I bought it, untried on my skin, after one whiff of it."

Kate and her games. Tricking him again.

"You always smell wonderful," he said.

"But this perfume is new and I did wonder if you'd even notice when I put it on. Maybe you need that little amulet of truth..."

Now, a day later, he had this appearance on his tongue in the bathroom vanity mirror.

Maybe the mark on his tongue was a trick of his mind and body, a mysterious appearance like *stigmata*, marks of bloodied hands and feet that appeared on certain devotees, matching the bodily wounds of Christ on the cross. A phenomenon thought by some to be psychosomatic in origin, though it was harder to explain away in the case of newborn babies.

This mark had to be a trick.

But maybe he was blaming the wrong trickster.

That was it. It was not his brain or his body punking him, he thought. It was his girlfriend Kate and her little games.

After the gin slings the night before, he'd probably been snoring with his mouth open, and Kate had playfully sketched the symbol on his tongue using a green eye-liner.

It was so Kate. She did that sort of thing. She'd once put lipstick on him during an afternoon doze, because she said he was asleep with a thoughtful pout on his lips. Which was fine, except that he'd hurried off to an engagement without checking his face beforehand.

And yet... Kate was a New Age adherent and for all her game playing she held an earnest respect for ancient Egyptian religion and its symbolism, more so than Daniel did these days.

Levity from her about ancient Egyptian symbols and mythology was surprising. Unless Kate thought he really needed a lesson about honesty.

Should he accuse her?

Right then she appeared in the doorway of their marble and brass bathroom.

"What about this sunhat on deck today?" she said, sporting a wide brimmed black hat that made a pool of her face.

"Honestly, the truth?" he said.

"What else?"

Daniel felt the feather image on his tongue meet the roof of his mouth.

"It makes your eyes look like an anxious crab's peering out from under a rock," he said.

"Too wide?"

A quick switch of hats to a grass one held in her other hand.

"This one?"

How could he tell her? How could he resist?

"Thatched umbrella."

A frown now.

"O-k-a-y... "

She left the doorway, came back with a red hat. She tipped her head down to show him that this one had a narrower brim, making a red circle of her head as she bent.

"Traffic stopper," he said.

"You like it."

"No. Makes me think of a traffic light. The red light that drivers in Cairo regard as optional. I'm not a fan of hats."

"You've never said that before. What's wrong with you?"

He wanted to reveal his secret then, show his tongue, but the mysterious mark had the feeling of a dreamworld gift and he was afraid of talking it away.

Maybe I'll just hold my tongue for a bit, he thought.

He couldn't simply blurt out what had just happened. He needed to know more about his affliction.

What was this strange blight affecting him? He'd been helpless to resist the urgings of his tongue in his response to Kate.

Auto suggestion?

What had suddenly come over him?

Truth?

In a post-truth world?

A late onset of truthfulness in life might not sound like a huge problem for most people. But it could be awkward for him, he thought.

Daniel Cane was an Egyptologist and a guest lecturer on a River Nile cruise. Trouble was, he was supposed to get along with passengers, not to mention his employer, a rich American who'd hired him. Calder Hall, an aging, vastly rich show-biz producer and sponsor of archaeology in Egypt.

Daniel had been invited to the man's presidential suite at the Mena House Hotel that overlooked the pyramids. The stone shapes looked grey and overbearing today, he thought, soaring hazard triangles that filled the balcony's view as he sat across from two men at a lacy wrought iron table.

The second man was the rich man's attorney, Hyman Robbins. Calder Hall waved dismissively at the pyramids spreading across the skyline.

"You couldn't stage this stuff, could you? Egypt - one big movie set." Calder was a shaven-headed octogenarian who immediately put Daniel in mind of the craggy mummy of Pharaoh Seti in the museum.

Daniel noticed a distinctive walking stick resting against the table, an antique Egyptian style stick with a golden jackal-dog's head that peered over the table. The dog's spiky ears were pressed back to smoothen the grip. Calder had suffered an early injury in a sports car accident and now walked with the aid of the mobility stick.

"I see you've still got Jack," Daniel said.

"Jack, my jackal-dog stick." He smiled. "You remember things, Daniel."

The walking stick had become a conversation piece when Daniel first met the rich champion of archaeology at a conference, about a year before.

"Isn't that Khentiamentiu, the early dog god of Abydos? Or maybe his other aspect, Wepwawet?" Daniel had said on that occasion.

"Very good," the old man had replied. "Most people just think Anubis, but of course Khentiamentiu and Wepwawet go back earlier as predecessors of Osiris the god of the dead."

"The Opener of Ways to the underworld," Daniel had said.

"That's it."

It had led to a discussion of a mutual interest in Abydos, Egypt's most ancient and holy burial ground, and a radical theory of Daniel's that the tomb of this canine-linked predecessor still remained to be found.

"I'll come to the point," the sponsor said now, turning his back on the view of the pyramids. "I want to hire your services as guest Egyptologist on a Nile cruise, but also as an investigator. The rewards will be greater than you could possibly earn in years of guest lecturing."

A few years away from the grind of guest lecturing, time to write more of those controversial books he longed to write and pursue those controversial theories he dreamed of pursuing, instead of playing ancient history tutor to fatuous groups of tourists in order to keep his 'body-and-ka' together as he termed it.

"Investigate?"

"Murder... mystery..."

"I'm an Egyptologist, Mr Hall," Daniel said. "Not a detective."

"I know. Call me Calder."

television programmes, Mr Hall is very involved in Egyptology as a generous sponsor," the lawyer put in.

"Don't I know it," Daniel said. "He's every Egyptologist's dream."

"Egyptology is my useless passion in life," the shaven-skulled patriarch took over. "Though not as useless as my family."

"So what am I supposed to do on this cruise?" Daniel said.

"Act the guest Egyptologist," the old man said. "Bring ancient Egypt to life for them. Just because there's murder afoot, doesn't mean the cruise has to be murder all the way. It's never too late for my ignorant family to learn something about my favourite subject of ancient Egypt. You'll emerge as chief of the investigation later on."

"But why me? You could click your fingers and a dozen Egyptologists would jump on board."

"I like your fresh and controversial ideas on Egyptology. The academics with tenures and big archaeological missions in Egypt tend to get stuck in the weeds of Egyptology, qualifying everything they say to avoid criticism, clever people, but always peering over their shoulders to check on peer approval."

"They don't even talk to me. I'm not linked with any university mission in Egypt you see."

"They talk to me, and I never even attended university. Self made."

"But you have money to sponsor their archaeological digs."

"Ah, yes. And I'll be sponsoring your crime dig as you probe below the surface for clues. Let me show you the setting for our murder mystery cruise."

Calder opened a golden laptop on the table, clicked a few keys and swung it around.

An antique white paddleboat on the Nile splashed across the screen.

"The *Belle Epoque*. And that's the era the vessel came from, but now spankingly refurbished inside. A luxury side wheeler steamer on a voyage up the Nile from Cairo all the way to Aswan, on the world's longest river. This will be the setting for your investigation."

A fantasy setting for a mystery murder game.

It had its appeal. But Daniel wasn't a crime detective in real life. He was an independent Egyptologist.

"Me as a detective?"

"Yes, unusual casting, but intriguing. I call it casting against type. Real detectives are drab and boring, I know. I have a brother who was once a police detective. But you, being an Egyptologist, will bring an archaeological flavor to your ponderings. And a refreshingly different approach. You'll be on a dig beneath the hidden layers for answers. It'll all become clear when we gather on board before for our cruise. And of course you are welcome to bring your lady friend along. It's the full cruise. What they call the '*six hundred mile Nile*'."

"I'm sure Kate would find it irresistible. She loves games."

Maat and her feather of truth

CHAPTER 2

A time of judgement

It was the first gathering on the river, the morning break, held in a sun-shafted Lounge that glowed on wooden panels and columns. After coffees, teas and Egyptian pastries, as the *Belle Epoque's paddle wheels* softly tramped along the Nile, the family members arranged themselves on leather couches and plush chairs.

The patriarch faced them in a tall backed chair, like a pharaoh's throne, his jackal-dog walking stick held across his chest like a sceptre of Egypt. At his side, a royal court official, his lawyer, sat in an upright chair.

Mayet, a young Egyptian filmmaker sporting an arty beret on her head, set herself up with her portable camcorder to capture the event. Daniel swept a glance over the family. He had only a brushing acquaintance with detective stories and was not as comfortable about evaluating potential suspects as he was Egyptian artefacts, but he understood that the first thing an investigator should do was to examine the cast of players and notice any quirks.

They did not appear to his eye to be an especially deplorable family at first glance, except for the youngest son, a brooding young man in his thirties, prematurely balding in the old man's image. The young man sat rudely fiddling with a laptop on his knee.

A computer addict who didn't care that his open lid and tapping keys announced to the world that he was bored and did not want to be part of this game.

Then there was 'the sisterhood', two long-haired women sitting close together, not twins, yet dressed in matching colours. Both were knitting. They reminded him of the twin goddesses Isis and Nephthys, who weaved the wrappings for the mummy of Osiris. Their defensive alliance clearly signaled: 'it's us against them.'

Next was the eldest son, Big Brother, his spreading legs laying a claim to the space around him, his bulk suggesting he would deserve the biggest share of everything, including the inheritance pie, Daniel thought.

Finally there was the family black sheep, Uncle Bryan, a grizzled ex-cop, who according to Calder was discharged for misconduct and repeated use of excessive force. He looked a hard man with tight skin across his cheeks and a controlled anger just beneath the surface.

The patriarch Calder Hall gave his family a probing inspection through stern, hooded eyes, before speaking.

"Here we are. Like a scene from the judgment in the Egyptian Book of the Dead. With Osiris presiding over the weighing of the souls against the Feather of Truth. And this *is* a time of judgement, because futures are in the balance. Yours. I'm taking a last look at you all before deciding about my Last Will and Testament. And I don't have much time because the time of my own judgment is approaching. I am hoping to recognize some glint of redeeming virtue in you.

But first, my strict rules. After this morning's get-together here, all personal phones and computers, except mine, will be surrendered and locked in the office safe of the Boat Manager until the end of the cruise. No contact with the outside world is permitted. Nobody is to leave until we reach the end, our terminus at Aswan on the last day of November. We're all sealed in rather splendid isolation, but then isolation is not so unusual in this post-pandemic age, is it? The boat will stop along the way at certain archaeological sites that interest me, for short excursions, but otherwise our group will remain isolated from the world, come what may.

The captain, crew and staff are contracted to follow this rule strictly and stand to be rewarded for their observation of our agreement. This is almost certainly my last cruise and I am planning a linear progression all the way up the Nile to Nubian Egypt in the heart of Africa, like a return to the beginning of time. Our first stop of interest is Amarna and our guest cruise Egyptologist Mr Daniel Cane will now give us a little background flavor and colour and the benefit of his fresh eye on Egypt".

The family remained in the Lounge for the onboard lecture.

Not out of any newfound passion for the 'Splendour that was Egypt', Daniel surmised.

They sat under the watchful eye of the old man.

Calder's assistant protégé, the young Egyptian filmmaker took up a spot where she could record Daniel and the audience members.

"Some shocking truths about Egypt. I used to love ancient Egypt uncritically, like a new religious convert," Daniel said at a lectern set up by a pair of stewards in their purple livery, caftans and tasseled *tarbooshes* in the 1920s Ottoman mode. "I still love it," he told his audience who faced the lectern in the comfort of soft chairs and couches. They were forced to sit together but there was an animosity in the room like a hostile courtroom. "Today I see the truth. Our first stop and site visit on this Nile cruise will disappoint you - especially those who went to visit the pyramids and Sphinx of Giza before we embarked. Anybody?"

No hands went up.

"Unlike Giza, there's not much to see at Tell-el-Amarna. A few broken columns and foundations on a plain and some royal tombs in the distant hills. But it's a site of controversy bigger than the pyramids themselves. Amarna, home of the heretic Akhenaten and his queen Nefertiti.

Here Akhenaten built his new city after abandoning the old gods of Egypt and the capital of Thebes for a brand new site of a city, which mushroomed in the desert like a nuclear test explosion. How did Akhenaten's whole new city come to be built on an empty plain in less than three years? Not a pretty story.

You recognize these two?" Daniel pressed a button and an image came up on a screen of the distorted eighteenth dynasty king Akhenaten and his elegant wife Nefertiti.

Akhenaten and Nefertiti

"Swan-necked Nefertiti, in the world famous sculpture that resides in Berlin's *Neues* Museum. She has an unmistakable quality of classic loveliness. But then she is not the only serene-looking First Lady in history, ancient or recent, who has adorned the arm of a psychopath. Nefertiti has only one eye in this image, you'll notice.

For me, it's history's supreme irony. Why? Because I believe the beautiful lady of Amarna was one-eyed, metaphorically speaking. She turned a blind eye on the horrors of what was going on at her new city.

Today it's fashionable for Egyptologists to claim that the pyramid builders were willing workers, perhaps the profession's agnostic reaction against the biblical whip and taskmaster scenes of epic movies. Yet the most casual glance at Egypt's monumental architecture tells us that ancient Egypt was no picnic for workers - whether they were prisoners, or Egyptians forced into state labour under the draconian *corvee* conscription system. Running away was a capital crime. Shirk and you could have your nose and ears cut off. Workers may not have been 'slaves' in name and they may have been fed by the state and had their injuries patched up by medicos, but coercion was at the core of Egyptian monumentality as new research reveals.

More shocking truth. There is evidence that Akhenaten used forced child labour, children uprooted from their families in Thebes hundreds of kilometres away and brought to build his city with little hope of returning. What proof? Burials of children and teenagers in disproportionate numbers in Amarna. More than ninety percent of the skeletons have an estimated age as low as seven, with the majority of these estimated to be younger than fifteen."

Was his audience horrified?

Not much.

Certainly not Computer Man, who still went on secretly fiddling with his laptop at the risk of his father's disapproval and at a risk to his chances of inheritance. Maybe he needed a last, urgent fix before they seized his drug of choice and locked it away for the rest of the cruise.

Daniel continued:

"Children provided a handy disposable workforce for the pharaoh's fanatical ambitions, yet despite their tender age at death, these skeletons were riddled with traumatic bone injuries and arthritis from heavy load bearing. It's no co-incidence that Akhenaten introduced new smaller stone blocks for building. Junior-size *Leggo* blocks known as *talatat*, to speed up the process. Instead of the cyclopean slabs used by his predecessors, these stones weighed seventy kilograms. Yet imagine hefting blocks of one hundred and fifty pounds all day long in the searing heat of Egypt's sun. Picture hordes of ill-nourished kids trying to manhandle them into place. Amarna may be a source of fascination to Egyptologists as the flowering place of a religious revolution and of a new artistic canon, but underneath, where the bodies lay, it was no Camelot, if you want the truth. Nor was Nefertiti as serene as she looked.

Nefertiti clubbing a victim to death in a smiting execution scene

Here's a scene from Boston Museum of Fine Arts that might surprise you." He flashed up an image of Nefertiti wearing her unique high crown.

"She still looks serene, but here she's holding a club in her hand and she's about to club a victim to death in a ritual execution scene.

The pharaohs were rather addicted to clubbing their enemies to death - in so-called smiting scenes of execution. Cracking skulls is probably the most persistently occurring image of pharaonic culture, but it's rare to see a queen poised in this menacing attitude..."

Daniel wrapped up his onboard lecture by concluding: "Incidentally, as a foreign Egyptologist in Egypt I am only permitted to provide lectures on board. By Egyptian law, licensed Egyptian tour guides must conduct group tours on sites. It's even frowned upon for a professional outsider to point at a ruin. Freelance Egyptian guides will be on the ground to help you. Any questions about Amarna?"

None from the family, but a comment from the patriarch.

"A refreshingly honest take on Amarna, Daniel," he said. "It's normally hallowed ground for Egyptologists."

Afterwards, as the passengers filed out, Daniel's girlfriend Kate was less then enthusiastic.

"How could you be so damning about Amarna and Ahhenaten?" she said.

"You mean how can I be an iconoclast about an iconoclast?"

"You're being odd."

"Maybe I'm finding a new streak of honesty. Do you suppose the truth about child labour in Amarna shocked our audience?"

"Worryingly, no. I heard some muttering that it was better than having youth violence and crimes on the streets."

"Law-and-order zealots. I wonder if they are going to be as caring about law and order in their own actions."

But of course this was only a game and they were playing the role of deplorables, he thought.

Quite convincingly though.

'Better lift my own game, he decided. 'Keep it real.'

Wasn't that the secret to successful acting?

"Let's get some air on deck," Kate said. "What do you say we go up and grab a sun-lounger?"

"You start burning without me. I'm going to stretch my legs."

The Egyptian Boat Manager, Mr Amira, advanced towards Daniel along the teak wood promenade deck, calling out a cheery "Good day, Sir," as Daniel approached him, adding: "Is everybody quite happy?"

"Convincingly, *no*, thank you" Daniel said. "But nobody could complain about your impeccable boat and service."

"Thank you, Sir," the round man said, smoothing away a flicker of puzzlement. "Do you happen to have your personal phone with you, Sir? We are collecting them."

'So the rules are going to apply to me, too,' Daniel thought.

"Yes, of course." He fished out an iPhone from a pocket of his cargo pants and handed it over with the twinge of unease he usually felt when parting with his passport to officials in Egypt.

"Any computers in your cabin, Sir?"

"None. I should be writing, I know, but no."

The Boat Manager placed the phone in a bag and moved on like a church usher going around with the offering basket.

"Thank you, Sir. Your phone will remain secure in my office, I assure you."

There weren't many passengers around. Maybe they'd gone to their cabins to collect their personal phones and computers before the round up.

Daniel approached the churning turmoil of a paddle wheel.

He paused on the deck above the side wheeler housing, felt the bite of the paddles in the water under his feet.

Dig, dig, dig...

That's exactly what he must do as a detective.

Start digging. Try to anticipate trouble before it happened.

The watery march of the rotating paddles in the blue-green Nile and the steady spray gave Daniel a reassuring sense of momentum, a hope that he was getting the feel of the situation.

But was it an illusion?

Questions churned in his mind.

Was everything as it seemed?

Was he being drawn into a cleverly staged game? Or dramatic reality?

Maybe both.

The rich producer may have hit on the idea of combining a mock drama with a real life one?

To what end?

To punish his feckless progeny and at the same time have the satisfaction of mounting one last ultimate production before he went out in a blaze of glory?

The old man had hired the young filmmaker to capture the event, after all.

The symbol of truth on Daniel's tongue touched the roof of his mouth.

True or false?

Egyptologists were expected to be skilled at discriminating between fakeries and the real thing. Like the swift judgement he'd made of the Maat amulet purchased from a street seller at *Khan el Kalili* bazaar. He'd dismissed it as a clever fake, but now he was beginning to wonder.

Was the family drama, taking place on the boat, fake or reality?

Reality?

Possibly reality television?

There was a startling thought.

Calder Hall was a big movie and television producer and it was not beyond the bounds of possibility that this whole affair was in fact a reality television show secretly being filmed and recorded under the cover of the girl's documentary.

Daniel inspected the deck and walls, seeking holes where hidden cameras and microphones might lurk, recording every step and word.

Was he under surveillance right now?

'I'm sure I don't look the part of a crime investigator,' he thought.

A casually dressed archaeology type in loose multi-pocketed clothing, with a field man's slouch, instead of the incisive figure of a Sherlock Holmes.

Yet big things were expected of him.

Clearly Calder Hall hoped that a trained archaeologist and Egyptologist might approach the challenge of a murder investigation in an entertainingly different manner. If Daniel failed, he might not only fail his employer, but also destroy any belief a television audience might have in the deductive abilities of Egyptologists.

'Ironic if I am the one carrying the flag for my profession', Daniel thought.

Stop it. You're being paranoid.

This is what it is.

A murder mystery game with an atmospheric cruise thrown in.

That's the truth of it.

Forget play-acting detective.

What would an archaeologist do?

First, he would pace out and survey the site and its topography.

Boots on the ground archaeology.

Daniel paced the seventy-two metre long vessel.

Broad passages linked lavish grand suites at either end and eighteen luxurious cabins in between, all air-conditioned and spread out over two decks, with a shaded sun deck up top.

Glints of gilding, brass, stained glass and shining, curved hardwood met the eye everywhere, as well as antique hanging photographs of early Egyptian royalty, along with European gentlemen archaeologists and their ladies under parasols. He passed through observation saloons, bars, the 1930s style lounge and a grand candelabra-drooped dining saloon below. He also noted a compact, book-lined library.

The *Belle Epoque* was a far cry from the mean streets of detective fiction, he thought.

A murder mystery game with an atmospheric cruise thrown in

CHAPTER 3

A smiting

After his tour, he went up to the sun deck to find Kate, who lay stretched out on a cushioned steamer chair, still reading her book on Egyptian mythology.

He watched the riverbank sliding by, palm bursts of trees among emerald green agricultural fields, with mountains replacing the outlines of pyramids in the distance.

"Were you relieved of your phone too?" she said, looking up.

"Yes."

"I can't even take photos now. I feel naked without it."

She was doing a pretty good job already in her handsome turquoise one-piece bathing suit, he thought admiringly.

He dropped into a deck chair beside her.

In spite of Calder Hall's faith in Daniel's investigative abilities, Kate's shrewd eye and instincts might be a valuable addition to his armoury. "What do you make of the players?" he said.

"I suppose our host's family is going along with this murder mystery idea to humour the old man."

"They're not doing it with much grace."

"And it's probably no fabrication that Calder Hall has a Will in real life and they hope to be part of it in the end."

"Yes, that's where the game thing blurs," he said.

"It's early,' she said, 'and depends on what parts in the drama have been assigned to them. But at face value, it's obvious to me that the family hates the old man as much as he hates them. In real life, I mean, not just in some made-up scenario. Nobody seems to be acting here."

Perceptive Kate.

He'd picked up mutual feelings of rancour too.

"You mean they're truly that horrible? Then they probably deserve each other."

"Karma," she said.

"Or Maat at work," he said.

"Maat! Yes, I've just been reading more about your Maat. The ancient Egyptian goddess of truth, balance and justice. There are similarities with Karma. The good and bad you do in your life comes to haunt you in your life to come."

Was it the good or the bad he had done that had brought these intimations of Maat into his life?

He sat back, tried to relax.

After the heaving clamour of Cairo's population and traffic, it was good to be on the timeless Nile again.

Kate waved her book on mythology.

"Who is your favourite Egyptian god or goddess?" she said.

"I'm intrigued by Khentiamentiu of ancient Abydos, who is symbolised by a jackal-dog."

"I'll pick Maat," she said, startling him. "The beautiful lady of truth. Maat's Egyptian priests were the judges of Egypt, I've learnt. They wore a golden emblem of Maat around their necks."

Yes, and they also bore Maat's emblem in another place, he thought, though it didn't appear in many books on mythology.

Ironic, he thought, that I have been put in the role of judging the guilty and the innocent in a murder mystery game. 'Maybe I should wear the Maat amulet I bought. Around my neck on a string.'

He pressed his tongue to the roof of his mouth. No, he didn't need a Maat necklace. He had her mark on his tongue already, the feather hieroglyph of truth.

"It says in here that Maat had Forty Two Laws that were the forerunners of the Ten Commandments," she said. "When the dead came to be judged in her weighing scales in the Hall of Maat, their hearts had to be lighter than a feather... free of all forty two sins."

"Some of those laws are almost identical to Old Testament ones," he said.

"Let's play a game," she said. "Imagine I'm Maat and you have to pass the test of my scales of judgement in order to survive in the afterlife." She flipped through to a page in her book. "Here. Answer me truthfully. Have you ever cursed anyone in thought, word or deeds?"

"Maybe a few hidebound Egyptologists."

"Have you ever stolen?"

"You mean used something in one of my books without proper attribution? Possibly, yes. I get tired of footnotes."

“Have you ever committed adultery?”

“I don’t qualify. I’m single.”

“No you’re not.”

“I mean unmarried.”

“Y-e-s. But would you?”

“Get married?

“Commit adultery if you were?”

“That’s not on Maat’s list. And no, I wouldn’t commit that sin, even if she was as attractive as you are in that bathing costume.”

“Seduced another man’s wife?”

“Never.”

“Falsely accused anyone?”

“I hope not. In fact I hope I don’t start. I’m expected to get things right in this investigation game.”

“Have you ever been an eavesdropper?”

“No, but I’m not above it.”

“Exaggerated your words when speaking?”

“Possibly in some of my archaeological theories, yes.”

“I don’t suppose you’ve ever stolen the god’s offerings?”

“Probably, yes. When I was a youthful volunteer on digs, no doubt. Archaeologists take ancient tomb offerings and put them in museums. How am I doing?”

“You may pass. Enter the heavenly Fields of *Aaru*, Justified One!”

“Thank you. ”

“Don’t you just love the goddess Maat?” she said.

"Yes, but I could be cynical and say Maat was an ideology that kept the pharaohs in power for so long. Maat stood for divine law and order. Don't rock the boat and risk overthrowing the old order. Keep the balance of status quo. But the laws of Maat applied to kings too. They were charged with the responsibility of preserving Maat, or universal order. Maat was the most important divinity in Egypt. She was the glue in their civilization and deeply revered. The greatest offering any pharaoh could make to the gods was to present them with an offering of Maat's image in miniature."

"Like the miniature amulet you bought the other day at *Khan el Kalili*?" she said.

He nodded.

"But in pure gold."

"May I see her again?"

'I don't have her on me,' he wanted to say, but he couldn't raise the lie to his tongue. He dug the green faience amulet out of a pocket and handed it over.

She admired the little figure in her palm.

"She's charming. Will you part with her? Look, she has a little loop here that I can slip onto a string necklace. The goddess Maat doesn't deserve to be hidden in the tomb of your pocket, Daniel. At least, if I'm wearing her, you will get to see her."

'And she will get to see me, watch me.'

Why was that faintly disturbing?

'Don't be superstitious,' he told himself.

"Keep her."

"Thank you. I'll wear Maat for you on the rest of the cruise."

The Egyptian filmmaker Mayet made an appearance on deck, camcorder in hand.

He'd first met Calder Hall's young protégé at the embarkation and he was attracted to her breezy Egyptian friendliness and humour. The girl had used her camcorder to capture the arrival of each of the passengers on board the *Belle Epoque*.

"This is a bit like the arrival scenes in the old Love Boat television series," she had joked to him at the time.

"Maybe 'Murder Boat'," he'd said...

"Hello Daniel, Kate. Am I interrupting you two? Sorry." She didn't wait for an answer. "Daniel, I'd like to do a piece with you talking to camera, recording your feelings about the set-up of our Nile show."

"You go ahead," Kate said to him. "I'm going back to the cabin to find a necklace string."

"Where shall we do it?" he said to the girl. "Do you want me looking like a detective or an Egyptologist?"

"Oh, Egyptologist is fine."

"Pity we don't have a background of ancient ruins and archaeological treasures," he said.

"I suppose that's where Egyptologists spend most of their time."

"No, in a library actually. And there's one on board."

"Perfect."

The library, lit by a picture window had a desk and a collection of books on shelves. While she looked around for the best set up, he remarked:

"Your name, Mayet. That's Egyptian."

"Yes, I am Egyptian, although I lived with my mother in America for a time."

"No, I mean ancient Egyptian," he said. "It's another spelling of the name Maat."

"You sound amazed."

Disturbed by the synchronicity of it, he thought.

First the amulet thing, then the mark of the tongue and a now a female namesake of Maat right here on board with him. Fantasy, mythology and reality were not merely bumping, they were dissolving into each other.

"I am a truth seeker, I suppose," she said. "I'm a filmmaker. So the name fits me."

She chose side lighting from the window and sat him in a chair near the desk, with rows of books behind him, popular Egypt titles, with their covers turned outwards: *The Egyptian Book of the Dead, Historical Atlas of Ancient Egypt. Egypt from the Air. Dictionary of Egyptian Civilization, Ancient Egyptian Magic...*

"Okay, please be honest and as frank as you can, Daniel," she directed him. "I want to capture the human aspect of this voyage. I want you, as an archaeologist, pondering, as if you've dug up a puzzle."

Be honest?

He had little choice.

THE CAMCORDER LENS FOCUSES ON THE RUGGED, BUT THOUGHTFULLY POUTING FACE OF DANIEL CANE, EGYPTOLOGIST.

HE BEGINS TO SPEAK IN A CONVERSATION WAY TO THE CAMERA.

HE HAS FRONTED DOCUMENTARIES BEFORE AND KNOWS TO MAKE A 100 PERCENT DELIVERY TO CAMERA FEEL INTIMATE AND CONVERSATIONAL.

"Truthfully, I am all at sea here.

Yes, even though this is the Nile and we're cruising the world's longest river.

I don't normally interrogate people, only facts and artefacts. I prefer the solitude of ruins, deserts, temples and tombs... and deserted libraries.

I seem to feel eyes on me all the time on this cruise. Maybe it's this camera.

A confession. The tragic pandemic worldwide lockdowns we look back on actually suited my temperament. Social distancing was something I habitually practiced, like most writers and theorists. Enforced Isolation for me was as if the rest of the world had suddenly caught up. Or slowed down, to match my life. But there's no social escape on a cruise boat of this size, even though it's half empty. Crew members outnumber the passengers.

A mock murder cruise in the Agatha Christie tradition was not something I would have put my hand up for, but it's all about mystery and mystery is what drives my interest in ancient Egypt. It's said that archaeologists and detectives are kindred spirits. The only difference being that, for an archaeologist, the parties of interest, as well as the witnesses, are all dead. Mind you, a few of the parties of interest could soon end up the same way if this should follow the pattern of an Agatha Christie plot.

What do I think of the line up?

"Tolstoy wrote: *'all happy families are alike; each unhappy family is unhappy in its own way'*. I think a more truthful pronouncement on families might be: *'all families are ugly in their own way'*. But are they murderous?" He shrugged.

"A bit, I suppose. Think of Thanksgivings and Christmases. Don't most families locked up together feel a bit like murdering each other after a while? And the family on this cruise has been given a massive motive."

That night the itinerary called for a thirties-style dress-up at dinner. A little jollity for a disgruntled family?

The boat manager provided a choice of costumes from an empty cabin turned into a dressing room, stocked with vintage costumes on hangars. Dresses, suits, feather boas, stoles, hats, coats, costume jewellery...

"A game within a game!" Kate said, her brown eyes shining. "Ooh, what fun! You've got to be a real detective tonight, Daniel. Poirot style. There's a grey three-piece lounge suit here and look, here's a black homburg hat."

"I hate hats."

"As you informed me. Now I'm getting my revenge. You have to throw yourself into playing a role."

"I thought I was playing a role."

"You've got to look the part. I fancy this green vintage frock to match my Maat amulet and maybe some sort of feathery hat or fascinator to go with it."

Feathers again.

The family played along, but that didn't mean they were going to play happy.

Dress-up had been mandated, so the family made a few concession to the occasion - a pith-helmet glumly worn on young Computer Man's head, headbands and sparkly evening outfits on the two sisters, a stuck-on Edwardian moustache drooping down the jowls of Big Brother. Uncle Bryan came dressed as a flashy thirties crime boss in a fedora, a black shirt and white tie and wearing big diamond cufflinks.

Calder arrived as a Lord Carnarvon type, echoing his role as a great patron of Egyptology. Legal Suit's concession to the informality of the evening was oiled back hair and a monocle.

"You look stunningly elegant, Kate, and that Fragrant Nefertiti fragrance is a hit."

"I didn't put any on."

"Yes, you did. Don't try to trick me again."

"Okay, I am wearing it tonight. Glad you like it."

Tonight? Was that a hint she'd worn it before? Or a playful tease?

Mayet, the young Egyptian filmmaker, stole the evening. She arrived in a pure white sheath dress, broad collar turquoise necklace and a headband surmounted by a tall white ostrich plume. Her light-caramel skin, dramatic eye-shadow and liquid dark eyes gave her a look that was both vintage thirties and ancient Egyptian in style, that peculiar convergence of the art-deco age.

Mayet had turned into Maat!

Startlingly so. Daniel's heart gave a kick.

The one jarring note was the camcorder bag

 I am being haunted by Maat, he thought.

Kate invited her to join their table.

"You are my favourite goddess," she said.

"And yet it is you, Kate, who wears the Maat necklace," the Egyptian girl laughed. "You look beautiful. And Daniel, look at you! You are the picture of the detective in the old Agatha Christie movies! Good evening, Hercule!"

"'Ercule, please."

"You should wear that suit when I film you."

"Not a moment longer than tonight."

"I will join you for dinner, thank you, but first I must take footage of the party..."

Mayet went off among the tables, stopping at each one to capture the moment and record individual comments of guests.

He tried not to stare.

Kate fingered the amulet on her necklace.

When Mayet returned to their table, she directed her camera on them.

"What a pair. The great detective and a lovely socialite. What do you make of the evening, Daniel?"

"It reminds me of tales of mythology and a story that begins: '*And all the dead who had died that day were gathered together on the Boat of Ra for their journey into the underworld...*' Fortunately, though, our murder mystery cruise has not produced any victims yet."

"And what do *you* make of this happy family gathering, Mayet?" Daniel said as she tucked her camcorder into its bag. "As an objective, outside eye on a curious family."

"Not a happy one to be part of I would think. And none of them very happy to be here. Except for Calder. But tonight I can forget them all for a moment and enjoy dinner with two favourite people."

"What's it like working for him?"

"Calder? As a young filmmaker, I feel under pressure from him. He watches updates of my footage at the end of each day. He seems to like my work, but I feel I am being judged of course."

"As am I. I'm sure you don't disappoint him. But I can't say the same for me, being cast as a detective."

"Casting against type. Calder likes doing that.

An eternity cruising the Nile

CHAPTER 4

The timeless Nile

Travel itineraries ought to be printed in blurred type, Daniel thought. They established a rhythm that ensured the days would blur together, the more pleasant, the more out of focus.

And the time on the river was surprisingly hazy and dreamlike.

For Daniel, each day of the cruise aboard the steam paddle wheeler *Belle Epoque* was like threading dazzling gemstones on an ancient Egyptian necklace, turquoise blue skies reflected in a blue-green Nile - shining days, glittering nights.

A circle of breakfasts, teas, lectures, lunches, sunset cocktails and opulent silver-service dinners in the dining saloon. Dinners were a feast, but not the spreading buffet feasts of yesterday, Daniel noticed. In the new mood of social distancing, spreading dishes and jostling buffet queues had lost their appeal. The tradition Egyptian favourites were all still there however, grilled Nile perch, fragrantly spiced lamb kebabs, falafel, hummus and eggplant dips.

And afterwards, nights spent between fine Egyptian linen in an antique brass bed.

Daniel began to relax as their paddle wheels ploughed the meandering upper reaches of the Nile.

The old man sought out Daniel as he stood leaning on the rail, viewing the pleasantly static diorama of Egypt that looked as it had looked for thousands of years, interrupted only by the sight of an occasional passing cruise ship like a floating hotel, and a stream of small, heavily-laden *feluccas* sailing by.

"Daniel, may I suggest a topic for another lecture? Abydos. The highlight of our cruise for me, and probably yours too. What about sharing your controversial theories about Abydos?"

"Do you think it would be interesting for the family?"

"If anyone can make it so, you can. Shock them with your honesty about ancient Egypt."

"Let's talk about murder, mass murder," Daniel began.

Interest stirred among the seated family in the Lounge. Was murder on their minds, or were they gruesome and ghastly?

"Egyptologists shrink from the subject, but in the earliest dynasties of Egypt, the king died and then people died. Particularly at Abydos, a highlight-stop of our cruise and the setting of countless murders. By that I mean the burial of royal subjects and servants who were forced to accompany a dead king into the afterlife. Egyptologists use the euphemisms 'subsidiary burials' and 'retainer sacrifices', but it was murder of the innocent. Perfect specimens. Young people, at the prime of their lives, killed and buried.

How did they die? They were not buried alive as some old movies suggest. Instead, archaeologists have found their bodies set out in an orderly fashion. None showed signs of mutilation or trauma on their skeletal remains as a result of say smiting their heads with maces in the pharaonic tradition. Some say these people died as a result of cyanide poisoning, others that they were strangled to death. Maybe their executioners borrowed from similar practices in neighbouring civilizations such as Sumeria, that show piercings into the skull cavity to the brain by a sharp instrument, possibly lifting an eye-lid to penetrate the brain, while leaving no trace. However it happened, the king's retinue and subjects joined him on a one-way journey to the underworld.

I'm talking about First Dynasty pharaohs like King Djer, the biggest culprit of such murders, his tomb buried in the deep sands of Abydos, overlooked by looming cliffs. Around Djer's vast single burial pit chamber with its internal chambers, lay satellite graves, honeycomb rows of cell-like cavities containing the bodies of three hundred and eighteen victims. Men and women. Perfect specimens. Reminding us of the 'unblemished beast sacrifices' of animals.

It was all about religious beliefs, yes, but also about status. You don't have great status in the afterlife if you don't have people under you to obey your every command.

In the Middle Kingdom of Egypt, a thousand years later, priests mistakenly declared the tomb of King Djer to be the tomb of the man-god Osiris, Lord of the Dead, and henceforth it became a site of pilgrimages and the setting for religious passion plays. Yet even earlier, Abydos was seen by the Egyptians as the site of the primary entrance to the underworld.

My controversial theory is this. There existed an earlier funerary god-king before Osiris, and his name was Khentiamentiu, depicted like Osiris as a man swathed in mummiform bandages, whose emblem was a standing jackal-dog. In fact, Osiris later absorbed his predecessor's attributes, which is why Osiris carried the epithet Osiris-Khentiamentiu. And Khentiamentiu was in turn associated with another jackal dog, Wepwawet, the 'Opener of Ways', but let's not get stuck in the weeds of Egyptology. Importantly, ancient Egyptians, and later Greek historians too, insist these god-kings actually existed, ruled in a golden age, and then were buried.

I theorize that Khentiamentiu lived and died and was buried at Abydos, along with the treasures of a man god, in a tomb possibly linked with the legendary entrance to the underworld. In fact, he may even share his tomb with the added burial of a Fourth Dynasty pharaoh Khufu, builder of the Great Pyramid of Giza.

A surprising suggestion?

Khufu's remains and treasures have never been found. His Great Pyramid chamber and coffin were found empty. Is it possible that Khufu changed his mind about the role of his pyramid at the last minute, as other pharaohs did, and instead had himself buried in the holiest site in Egypt, Abydos, leaving his empty Great Pyramid as the world's largest memorial cenotaph? You see, no statue has ever been found of king Khufu at Giza, site of his pyramid. Only one small ivory statue of Khufu has ever turned up. In... yes, you guessed it, Abydos!

Perhaps a bit of a stretch, this part of my theory, but a teaser.

Why haven't archaeologists found Khentiamentiu's tomb-of-all tombs?

The singing sands of Abydos are probably to blame.

Singing sands? The desert here produces an eerie sound when the wind blows over it, said to be caused by the peculiarly fine, *aeolian* sand. Others say the singing is a ghostly echo of the mourning and jubilation of ancient pilgrims, processions of worshipers who over the centuries reenacted the funeral rites of Osiris.

The sands of Abydos are deep. 'You don't clear it away with a brush', as one archaeologist put it. Ground-penetrating radar hints at other hidden structures, but mainstream Egyptology rejects my theory about Khentiameniu. Maybe, one day..."

Calder Hall tapped his stick on the floor in solitary applause at the end.

"Thank you, Daniel. Maybe one day you'll find the key that will shake up the old Egyptology community."

The *Belle Epoque* paddle wheeler stopped at *Minya* and the group went ashore to visit *Tel El Amarna,* in pursuit of what travel brochures called the 'Amarna Experience'. But the empty plain of Amarna, abandoned after just seven years to the winds and the wolves, or at least the jackal-dogs, was an experience of desolation, a vanished empire of the imagination set in sepia sand, as Daniel described it.

Their Egyptian tour guide on the site swept an arm across the view of the plain.

"Here Pharaoh Akhenaten built his brand new city and worshiped his sole god, Aten, whose symbol was the shining disk of the sun."

When that failed to impress the family, he added: "We are standing on the historic plain of Amarna."

"Plain boring, if you ask me," Computer Man said in a mutter.

Calder's family members were not worshipers of the sun. They scowled in the dazzling Amarna heat. Where were images of swan-necked Nefertiti and mad king Akhenaten?

"You will see them in the tombs," the guide pointed.

But where were the palaces and sun temples? Where was the city?

Tomb images of Akhenaten and Nefertiti

On the following morning, the stringed turquoise necklace of their cruise itinerary snapped and the gems scattered around the decks of *Belle Epoque* like the shock of a jewel robbery.

The old man Calder Hall, host of their cruise, had gone missing.

News flew around the boat.

The vessel had slipped its mooring early in the morning before the passengers stirred and Calder had not been missed until later in the day. Perhaps the old man had slept in after a stirring folkloric dancing show on board that night, performed by the crew, and the drinking that had continued later.

At least that was what people assumed.

Now the old man was gone.

But how could he disappear?

The lawyer Hyman Robbins broke the news to Daniel on a flying visit to their cabin, the young Egyptian filmmaker in tow, clutching her camcorder.

CHAPTER 5

The dig begins

"What do you want to do?" Legal Suit said to Daniel.

"Do?"

"You're in charge."

"Of?"

"The investigation."

"Ah, yes. Investigation. We must investigate. I think the boat should be searched from stem to stern."

"We've done that."

"Then do it again. More thoroughly this time. Calder's playing a game, but I hardly think he'd jump overboard in the spirit of it. No, he's found a secret hiding place somewhere and won't reappear until we've found his killer."

"Then you think - "

"We're playing a game, right?"

The lawyer gulped.

"How do I put this? It's not the best time to break it to you, but this is not entirely a game. In fact, not a game at all. The only game was letting you believe that this was to be a mock murder cruise. My client's misdirection. He wanted you to discover the truth for yourself. Mr Hall liked putting people into situations, as I tried to warn you."

A gravitational pull took hold of Daniel's body. It felt as if the *Belle Epoque* had suddenly gone into reverse, back-paddling furiously.

"So it's real and not some reality production."

The *Belle Epoque* kept going straight ahead, while Daniel's mind went on lurching.

"It's reality, and yes, it could be defined as quite a production," the lawyer said.

"I told you nobody seemed to be acting," Kate said in a murmur to Daniel.

"Calder's last great production," Daniel said.

"You might say that," Legal Suit said.

"And now he's gone missing?"

"Yes. So what procedural steps do you wish to take?"

"I suppose we should talk to the family."

"But should we not return to our last stop? In case Mr Hall got off the boat unobserved, perhaps in the quiet hours? Or fell overboard?"

If Calder had fallen into the River Nile he could be miles downstream by now. Should they turn around and start combing the river?

It sounded futile to Daniel.

"First we bring the family into this."

"Which of you was the last one to see Calder last night?" Daniel said.

The family, assembled in the Lounge, stood around in a defensive semi-circle.

Nobody responded.

"C'mon Craig. We heard Dad ask you to help him with his computer last night," the elder sister said.

"Okay, I admit. I saw him late last night."

Computer Man.

"I went with him to his suite. He was having computer problems, his programmes and apps crashing. I said it was late and I'd take his machine back to my cabin to look at, but Dad stuck to his rules. No access to computers or phones, except his. He made me fix the problem while he breathed down my neck. It didn't take me long."

"How long? What time did you leave his suite?"

"Around midnight. He was fine when I left him."

"You would say that," Big Brother said in an accusing tone. "But why would you do such a dumb thing to him?"

"Maybe he's in debt again and wanted to fast track his inheritance, if he's stupid enough to think he's getting one," a sister suggested.

"Yes," the other agreed. "Maybe he hasn't been able to hack any bank accounts lately. He's prison population, our baby brother."

"At least I shared some of it with you, when you two needed money."

"Shared what wasn't yours."

"Why would I do anything to Dad, especially when you heard him ask me to go to his cabin to fix his computer?"

"You're brazen, like all cons."

But where was the motive to harm the father?

The Will? Computer Man's behaviour had not been that of someone expecting, or deserving, an inheritance. He'd ignored the onboard lectures his father had arranged for the family, blatantly displaying a total lack of interest in proceedings.

Was it revenge that drove him to it? Anger at his father?

'Something doesn't quite click,' Daniel thought.

His next step would be to visit the possible scene of the crime.

The old man's luxury suite.

Legal Suit and camera-girl accompanied him.

Wooden-framed picture windows in the sumptuous suite gave panoramic views of the Nile ahead and challenged the notion of a death scene. 'Jack' the jackal-dog walking stick was still here, propped against an antique table, standing guard over the suite, so the old man hadn't slipped ashore. He would never have gone anywhere without his stick.

The bed lay unused.

A thumbed copy of *Death on the Nile* sat on his bedside table.

Bottles of gin, whisky and a selection of fine ports stood on a silver tray on a dresser. The old man's golden laptop computer sat open on an antique desk. Wouldn't Calder have closed the lid if he'd finished with it?

Maybe.

Daniel wondered about the computer and what it might tell. Calder was a dying man. He might have fallen prey to depression and revealed something.

Daniel started up the machine.

"A suicide note, I wonder?" he said.

The computer flashed into life and asked for a password.

"Can't get in. Maybe a dead end anyway. The old man was enjoying himself far too much on the *Belle Epoque.*"

Calder had also been keen to fulfill his dream of reaching Abydos and then going on to the destination of Aswan and completing a last 'linear progression' up the Nile - although he probably guessed he would never make it all the way.

There was no sign of a struggle or disturbance in the suite, let alone blood.

What next?

"Okay, we'd better turn the boat around now and head back to the other possible scene of the crime. The riverside mooring where he was last seen," Daniel said.

"I'll inform the Boat Manager," Legal Suit said.

An old man's body had been found on the riverbank, enquiries by the Boat Manager discovered from local villagers. Had he been in the water? A little hard to tell. He was dry after lying there in the heat of the day. Perhaps somebody had spotted the body and dragged it ashore, looking for money.

Daniel, the lawyer and the filmmaker Mayet joined the ship's doctor, a Coptic Egyptian, in the boat's white medical clinic area where the body lay under a sheet on an examination table, hidden behind a screen.

"He did not drown," the doctor explained. "He was clubbed to death with something blunt. See, here." The doctor pulled back the sheet. Daniel had been up close and personal with ancient Egyptian mummies, so death no longer frightened him, yet it was a relief not to be met by the bloodied face of the dead man. Instead, the sponsor of archaeology had been turned onto his stomach to display his back and a view of multiple blows to the old man's bald crown, back of the head, neck and spine.

Blows had rained down on him.

A scene of a wall carving flashed into Daniel's mind of a pharaoh clubbing his enemies to death, but if this had been the work of a single executioner then he must have struck in an unhinged fury that seemed excessive.

Multiple attackers?

Daniel pictured a Julius-Caesar style execution with the whole family, like a ring of conspirators, raining blows on Calder's head and body.

Was it possible?

A joint murder?

A rare moment of family togetherness?

Mystifying.

"What now?" the lawyer said.

"There's no playing around any longer. Call in the police and call off this cruise."

"That's not in the agreement." The lawyer shook his head. "You are in charge of the investigation, as stipulated, but I am enforcing the terms of the agreement solemnly drawn up with everybody on board and I will not be neglecting my deceased client's instructions. Mr Hall intended the cruise to complete its journey up the Nile, come what may. And that is precisely what we shall do. Therefore nobody must leave the cruise and the cruise must continue as planned. We are just at the beginning."

Legal Suit.

It might have sounded like a bizarre idea to honour a dead man's cruise itinerary, but not so peculiar to an Egyptologist like Daniel. After all, mummies of ancient Egypt's wealthy classes customarily embarked on *post mortem* journeys by boat along the Nile. They made a pilgrimage to the holy site at Abydos, traditionally believed to be the burial ground of the god Osiris, Lord of the Underworld and Judge of the Dead, before being returned to their home city for final burial.

"But what about the body?" he said.

"We have a spare chill room, largely empty with such a small passenger list on the cruise," the doctor said.

"We continue, as normally as possible," Legal Suit said. "In fact, tomorrow morning I am bound to read out the first part of my deceased client's Will." How smoothly the lawyer's description of Calder Hall slipped from 'client' to 'deceased client'.

"You're going through with this? All the way?"

"As indeed you must, too, in order to receive the full sum of your fee, according to the agreement we struck."

Bad Cop Uncle Bryan cornered Daniel on deck.

"Do you know what you're doing, Mister Archaeology Excavator? I thought you might be walking around with a shovel."

The descriptor made Daniel feel he should be wearing a hard hat.

Ex-cop Uncle Bryan clearly thought as a former detective he was the experienced one who should be put in charge of the investigation.

"We don't often use shovels in archaeology. Mostly a small, flat trowel," Daniel said in reply.

The tight skin over Uncle Bryan's cheeks grew tighter.

"Have you made a proper investigation of the crime scene? Gone over my brother's suite and collected all the evidence?"

"Brushed the place over with powder for fingerprints? No. We prefer using brushes to dust off dirt in archaeology."

"A crime scene can tell you a lot, if you know what you're looking for. You want some tips?"

"About who did it, sure."

"About doing your job. Maybe you should step aside and let a pro head up the investigation."

"I'm afraid you're disqualified."

"What have they been telling you about me? I was wrongly discharged."

"You're disqualified because you are a member of the family and must be seen as one of the suspects."

The grizzled man laughed with an unpleasant wheeze.

"So we're all suspects! How do you know some crew member didn't do it?"

"Do you know how important the tourist trade is to Egyptians, how much they've suffered without tourism in the past?" Daniel said. "The crew nearly kissed us all when we came on board. No, I don't think this crew is going to be killing anybody."

"You think I'm a suspect? You think a good cop is going to do a stupid stunt like kill someone in a lock-up?"

"Maybe not a good cop. I've been put in charge. Your brother was quite specific about it."

"I hope you've secured the crime scene. Once it's tampered with it's never the same."

That was true of archaeology too, Daniel thought. Archaeology was a destructive profession. Once you'd dug up and disturbed a site, it stopped telling you things.

"I haven't put crime scene tape around the suite, if what's what you mean, but yes, the suite is now off limits."

"Any sign of forced entry?"

"The door was unlocked at the time."

"Anything in his trash bin? In his bathroom?"

"Bathroom?"

"Clues. Wet towels, cloths, signs of a clean up? Was the toilet seat left up?"

"What does that prove?"

"Old guys leak a lot. We tend to leave the seat up all the time. So if the seat's down, a lady might have used it. Or ladies. We'd all been drinking a lot. Did you even notice?"

"Thanks, but I'm the one supposed to be asking questions."

"About that. When are you going to start proper Investigative interviews?"

"We try not to rush things in archaeology."

"I haven't noticed you doing any surveillance, either. Secretly hiding and watching suspects for suspicious behaviour."

"Then I've been successful."

Uncle Bryan apparently expected Daniel to go behind potted palms and aspidistras in a surveillance operation.

"You gotta build a case, Buddy."

Archaeologists didn't build cases, they built narratives about people and mythologies of the past, Daniel thought, but it was a fine point of difference Uncle Bryan might not appreciate.

THE VIDEOCAM SHOWS THE FACE OF THE YOUNGEST MEMBER OF THE FAMILY IN CLOSE-UP. HE RESENTS THE SCRUTINY.

"I wasn't the last one of us to see my father alive. Somebody else was. The one who killed him. Just because I went to Dad's cabin late in the night doesn't prove anything. I was helping him, more than the others ever did. What about my big brother? He was always throwing his weight around. Or my weird and creepy sisters who sit there all day with their balls of knitting wool and needles going clickety clack. Mixing colours like witches stirring potions.

If I hadn't discovered computer games as a kid, my family would have driven me bat-shit crazy. But you can't dump my father's death on me."

THE VIDEOCAM CAPTURES A LARGE MAN WHO FILLS A DECKCHAIR AS WELL AS THE LENS.

"What has little brother been telling you? The one whose favourite words as a kid were always: "I didn't do it! It wasn't me!" It usually was.

Or my craft-loving sisters that my father underestimates. They've got clever fingers, but they're also manipulative. I wouldn't put it past them to do something.

Two of them could have pulled it off together and I can't really blame them for hating him, the way he treated them.

The way he treated all of us.

No, that doesn't mean I hated him enough to kill him. But as the eldest, I suppose I should have done more to protect the old man. From us."

THE VIDEO CAM SHOWS TWO WOMEN, SISTERS, ENGAGED IN MAKING A BALL FROM A SKEIN OF BLACK WOOL, USING THE ONE'S SPLAYED HANDS AND THUMB AS A WINDING ARM. THEY PAUSE MOMENTARILY TO SPEAK TO THE CAMERA.

"It doesn't make a lot of sense to kill our father –"
"– not if we're supposed to be on this cruise to make a good impression on him. So he'd put us in his wool –"
"– Will, she meant."
"Tragic business."
"Awful. But men can be violent. Our brothers have a lot of anger issues.
We never did impress our father and I don't think we succeeded on this cruise. But we didn't kill him."

THE VIDEOCAM INTERROGATES THE TIGHT, ANGRY FEATURES OF A GRIZZLED MAN. HE GLARES DOWN THE LENS.

"That tomb digger guy! He's an investigator without a clue. And you know what? He's not going to find one either. You don't get to understand crime investigation by watching CIS or remakes of Agatha Christie murders. Death on the Nile? Ha Ha. I'll tell you about a death. That Egyptologist is going to kill this investigation. Why hasn't he hauled everybody aside for questioning, one at a time? Does he even know the techniques of interviewing suspects? People are tricky, slippery things. They don't just lie there under your magnifying glass."

THE VIDEOCAM SEES EGYPTOLOGIST DANIEL CANE PACING THE CONFINES OF THE SMALL ON-BOARD LIBRARY, THE CAMERA PANNING WITH HIM.

"So here it is, the last production of Calder Hall. I suppose I should be grilling the family for clues - creating some dramatic Interrogation scenes for your camera. Following the standard criminal investigation process we see in movies. But to me that feels like taking the artefact out of its context before I've properly studied or recorded it within its context - and that context here is the family. I think that in forming my impressions I should look at them *where they are* in their family strata, observing the group dynamics rather than putting them in a lab for microscopic study.

I don't think I was hired to turn this into a police procedural story.

If I was, then they're going to be as disappointed as Uncle Bryan."

Nile village

CHAPTER 6

A malignant Will

Before the afternoon break, Daniel took himself to his favourite thinking place above a churning paddle wheel. The turn of the wheel seemed to impel his thinking and encourage a sense of progress. Today the rotating paddles in the water produced a different sound to Daniel's ear.

Shit, shit, shit.

Who'd have picked the father to be a victim, and so early?

He leaned against a rail and gazed out at a riverbank view of passing farmland where workers toiled at their plots. Not much in rural Egypt had changed over the centuries. Donkeys trotted along the bank, dwarfed by sheaves of watercress on their backs. A *fellaheen* raised water to his irrigation canal. Some farmer still used a *shaduf,* an ancient Egyptian invention involving a bucket hinged on a lengthy pole to lever up water, but this one used a cow to turn a vertical water wheel, a kind of paddle wheel with clay pots strapped to the outside rim that scooped up water and deposited it in gushes at a higher level, a device introduced in the Roman period.

Yet another turning paddle wheel, Daniel thought, like a sort of mechanized bucket brigade.

Splash, splash, spash.

For some reason he pictured the dead man's family working in unison in a bucket brigade, the bedeviling idea returning that they had all somehow combined to club him to death, each armed with a weapon.

Bash, bash, bash.

Wheels within wheels turned in Daniel's brain.

Why kill the old man at all?

THE VIDEO STREAM FINDS EGYPTOLOGIST DANIEL CANE BACK IN THE LIBRARY OF THE *BELLE EPOQUE,* ADDRESSING THE CAMERA.

"Shocking fact has overtaken fiction. What was presented to me as an entertaining mystery game has suddenly turned into a very deadly one. My host and employer, and the patriarch of the family, has turned out to be an unexpected victim.

Egyptology is all about death. Death was the testator that bequeathed us our knowledge of the ancient Egyptians, and did so in a profusion and richness unmatched by any other ancient civilization.

But death is a shock in the here and now. No less for me. Yet I don't see much grieving going on here. There are none of those scenes of a family holding up their arms to the skies in mourning that we see painted on the walls of tombs, no hired female mourners wailing and throwing the dust of anguish onto their

**hair. This group is more like vultures circling, hungry to swoop
and gorge on a carcass.**

Death in Egypt

Morning coffees and teas served in the Lounge was more like a
wake.

If this was not a contrived murder mystery, then it followed the
tropes.

A death, followed by a Reading of the Will to an undeserving,
assembled family. The family and the lawyer sat in a semi-circle of
soft chairs and couches. Kate sat aside.

Mayet, the Egyptian girl, positioned herself to record events on her
camcorder.

It was amazing how quickly she blended into the scenery, in spite of
her jaunty beret.

Legal Suit, Hyman Robbins, addressed them, opening an envelope
with none of the fumbling that occurred at academy awards
ceremonies.

"The Last Will and Testament of Calder Hall..." he announced, then paused to scan the standard legalese. "I won't hold you in suspense with the preliminaries about the Executor... *me*... and about *my* total powers as the Executor, etcetera... I'll move to the Disposition of the Estate." He frowned here. "But a note of warning." He shifted uncomfortably in his chair. "This document breaks with the pattern by including some informal opening statements. It's an address by Calder Hall to you all."

Hyman Robbins looked over his reading glasses at them, cleared his throat and read out his dead client's words:-

"I had thought of opening this preliminary statement to you, my surviving family, with six words.
Go to hell, all of you!

Or maybe, more colourfully, opening with a pronouncement of an ancient Egyptian curse...

May you all lose your earthly positions and honors.
May you capsize and drown in the Nile, have no successors, receive no tomb or funerary offerings of your own, and your bodies decay because you will starve without sustenance and your bones perish."

Daniel found himself warming to the now cold Calder Hall.
He gave an involuntary chuckle, which made him rattle his coffee cup in its saucer. Kate bumped his knee and frowned in disapproval.
The old patriarch's broadside hardly surprised the family.

Perhaps they expected contempt from him.

But a curse?

Calder Hall clearly guessed he was going to die some time along this cruise and was unlikely to reach the end, Daniel thought, though he may not have quite expected his own murder.

Legal Suit continued the reading.

"However, I can't take it all with me as they say, unlike my beloved Egyptian pharaohs, who buried their riches in tombs alongside their mummies. So here is my Will... or the first part of it." The lawyer paused for dramatic effect. "Who receives inheritance in the Estate? Only ONE, to be named in a second reading of a codicil at the end of the cruise. Only ONE party shall receive benefits from my estate - the entire inheritance - effective from the final day of the cruise. However, should the undisclosed beneficiary fail to survive to the last day of the cruise, as a result of some unforeseen circumstance, then the family shall all share EQUALLY in the inheritance. Note, if any beneficiary under this Will contests any of the provisions of this Will, then each and all such persons shall not be entitled to any devises, legacies or benefits under this Will or codicil hereto... Furthermore, the cruise must go on, whatever occurs, as the Captain and crew have been instructed. If you do not reach Aswan on the due date, the provisions of Distribution will be cancelled and the entire estate awarded to archaeology."

One member would receive ALL of the estate?

'Interesting twist,' Daniel thought.

Also alarming.

Fail to survive to the last day of the cruise, as a result of some unforeseen circumstance?

Ominous.

The father planned to set the family at each other's throats. If they truly were as vile as the dead man suggested, then this reading of the Will could turn the gracious *Belle Epoque* into a gladiatorial arena.

"Only one to inherit? This is a bad joke, right?" Big Brother said.

"*One?*" the close-knit sisters said as one, dropping their knitting.

The family swung accusing looks at each other. All except Computer Man, who sat, disinterested as always, legs crossed as if to accentuate the absence of his confiscated laptop that he had so compulsively fiddled with earlier. Maybe it was resignation in his attitude. If only *one* party would inherit from the father, it wouldn't be him.

Who was the 'chosen' one?

The Sisterhood fixed their stare on the bulk of Big Brother.

"It's you, isn't it, Leo," the elder sister said accusingly to the brother.

"That's right - give it all to the eldest male!"

"Yay, go the patriarchy!" the other sister cheered caustically.

A potential beneficiary might have shown satisfaction at being tipped by his siblings as a favoured one, but Big Brother looked as if he'd been fingered and was uncomfortable about taking the heat, despite the air-conditioned surroundings of the boat Lounge. He used a blunt finger to loosen his collar.

"That's bull. Dad had no time for me, and if he was just going to
follow a traditional form of choosing the eldest son, then why drag
all of us here to this goddamned place?"

Daniel couldn't resist making a dig.

"Maybe it's another hidden legacy," he said. "An educational
experience to pass on his love of ancient Egypt to you all."

If it was a legacy, then it was not one they valued.

"Thanks Dad –" the sisters addressed the absent father loudly.

"– for nothing!"

"We've got the History Channel at home if we wanted ancient
history," Big Brother said.

"You won't find too much of it there," Daniel said. "Ancient
Aliens..?"

Was this the start of more mayhem?

Daniel still had to address the death of the father - and the sight of
Bad Cop Uncle Bryan glowering from his chair challenged him.

After the reading of the Will, Daniel stood up.

Big Brother snorted.

"You think we're going to sit here and listen to a lecture on ancient
history? We don't have to humour the old man any more."

"Not a lecture," Daniel said. "But you may want to listen to what I
have to say. I know how your father died."

That got their attention.

Everybody's.

Including Computer Man's.

And especially Bad Cop's.

"You know?" the sisters said.

"We all know how he died," Bad Cop said in a weary voice. "The doctor's report said he got hit on the head."

"Yes," Daniel said, "and on the back of the head and on the neck and along the spine. A thicket of clubs falling on him one after the other," he said, sweeping them in a glance.

"You think we ganged up on our father?" the Sisterhood said.

"It did occur to me, I must be honest," Daniel said. 1q

"We're women. Women don't club people to death."

"No? Nefertiti did. But I think there's another explanation."

"Please continue," Legal Suit said.

"Those club wounds on Calder Hall's body are the result of bludgeoning caused by rotating paddle wheels, striking his body one after another. It must have happened when the boat left the mooring early yesterday. The paddle wheel sucked him underneath."

"Then that's how he died," Computer Man said.

"Not necessarily. One of those blows, the initial deadly one, comes from his killer, I believe. That's why your father didn't drown. He must have been dead before he hit the water. Struck on the head with a heavy object, which I now suspect, after checking the suite's liquor bar inventory, was a missing bottle of vintage tawny port. His body was then tipped over the bow into the water, probably in the expectation that it would float away in the current. But somehow his body snagged under a paddle wheel where it took a sustained beating in the morning."

"A missing bottle of port doesn't prove anything," Computer Man said.

"The kid's right. A cabin cleaner could have taken the bottle," Uncle Bryan added.

"Muslims don't drink," Daniel said.

"But how can you prove foul play if he had so many bangs on him?"

"He didn't drown, remember."

"He may have banged his head and died on the way down as he fell overboard somehow," Computer Man said.

"Admittedly, yes, it would be hard to prove my theory. That's why whoever performed the deed, walks free for now. They're among us. But this is a lock-up, luxurious as it is, so they're not going anywhere."

"So what are we supposed to do, carry on paddling up the river as if nothing's happened?" Big Brother said.

Legal Suit harked back to the terms and conditions.

"The rules still apply. The cruise must continue, come what may. Or nobody inherits."

"I've got a question for you, Mr Egyptologist," Big Brother said.

"How well did you know our father?"

"Know?"

"Were you confidants? We know the lawyer Hyman Robbins. He's been the family lawyer for decades and our father's guarded confidant, but why are you here?"

"I'm a guest Egyptologist."

"Our father bankrolled Egyptology. He must have known plenty of Egyptologists, many who'd worked with him. He was also a man who never did things by accident. Why choose you? Maybe you know what was going on in his mind because Hyman Robbins here certainly won't tell us. So we ask again, how well did you know him?"

"I met him once at a conference. Before he hired me for the cruise. Maybe you should be asking how well he knew you. Too well maybe? Or enough to know that somebody here, the lucky one who gets the pharaoh's treasure, if he or she survives the cruise, possesses some claim to virtue the rest of you don't?"

Daniel, the lawyer, and Kate, left the Lounge.

The family remained, silent, in a state of bemusement

On an impulse, Daniel stopped at the door to linger outside.

"You go on," he said.

"You're going to eavesdrop?" Kate said.

"I told you it's not beyond me."

"You're supposed to be playing detective, not spy."

He placed a finger to his lips.

The two left.

Daniel flattened himself against a paneled wall to listen. Nothing. The soft chug of the steam engine vibrated through the vessel's interior. Was it drowning out their voices?

No, they'd been stunned into silence.

Somebody spoke.

Computer Man's voice.

"You know what? I've got a suggestion, a solution that might stop us all squabbling for hundreds of miles. We've got a lawyer on board. Let's draw up an agreement that whichever family member gets named as the sole heir at the end of the cruise they will waive their right and agree to share the inheritance equally among all of us."

Desolate emptiness ensued like the sound of crickets at night.

Stupefaction at the simplicity of the suggestion? Daniel wondered.

Not for long.

"There you go again, splashing around money that isn't yours to give," a sister said.

"Think about it. Doesn't it sound fair?" the young brother said.

"Not a bad suggestion, Kid," Bad Cop said.

"Easy for you to say," Big Brother said.

"Yes, who thinks you're even in the running?"

"Little brother is scheming – "

"– as always," the Sisterhood said.

What kind of family was this? Were they that greedy?

Evidently this family didn't do fair. It was eminently fair in Daniel's view, in fact it had a surprising touch of reasonableness, even generosity.

Silence again.

Daniel heard the scrape of a chair.

They were coming out.

He left.

VIDEOCAM CAPTURES DANIEL LOOKING PENSIVE, NOT ENTIRELY PLEASED WITH HIMSELF. HE IS ON DECK FROWNING IN THE BRIGHT LIGHT, LISTENING TO THE REGULAR BEAT OF THE PADDLE WHEEL.

(Young Female voice, off camera, speaks with a faint Arabic accent:)

"What are you thinking and feeling, Daniel? Are you satisfied with your work on the investigation?

"I'm satisfied with my hunch about the paddle wheel blows, but my thoughts are still spinning. I still don't understand a lot of things. Who killed the father? Why? Why so early on in the cruise?

Do I, as an Egyptologist and archaeologist, have special tools that I can bring to the investigation?

Digging, sifting the clues, establishing context, dating and interpreting them, classifying them, analysing, deciphering and preserving them, recording every steps of the progress, which you are apparently doing for me on camera...

In archaeology, artefacts emerge in front of your eyes and you can see them. The detective can't be sure if what he's looking at is a clue. Anything around him could be a clue.

I suppose my next step is to get underneath the hidden layers of the suspects. But instead of interrogating them one on one, I might try a different approach. After dinner tonight..."

River Nile, passing scenery

CHAPTER 7

Quiz Night

It was a muted dinner in the dining saloon, with only murmured conversation, accompanied by the clink and tinkle of silver cutlery on fine bone china.

 It was time to dig beneath the surface layers, Daniel thought. You had to break ground to find the truth.

The family had chosen separate tables, he noted. No togetherness in grief tonight.

Daniel stood.

"Your attention, please, diners. Our Nile cruise itinerary declares an after dinner entertainment this evening. It's Quiz Night!" He looked around with a wan smile. The family looked back appalled. They hadn't signed up for party games, in spite of Calder Hall's couching the cruise to Daniel as a mock murder mystery. "Quiz Night suggests trivia questions, or general knowledge, but I want to do something more specific. I want to quiz you about your rnship with your father. Instead of interrogating each of you, tied to a chair under a naked light bulb, we'll do this in a more comfortable setting, right here, over glasses of vintage port, which I see is now being served."

Liveried stewards spread through the dining saloon filling Edwardian style glasses.

"I want to ask each of you: what was your relationship with your father?"

They took shelter behind their ports.

"Do I have to nominate a family member? Come on now, who's first? You don't have to get up on your feet."

Eyes avoided his.

Big Brother put down his port.

"As the eldest son, I suppose I should take the lead."

That got a stare, but tension eased around the saloon.

Big Brother looked a little damp, fearful.

Not of Daniel, or the quiz, it appeared, but of his audience, the attentive family, a fear which he betrayed through uneasy, sidelong glances.

He was afraid of his own family.

Was it perilous to be popular, to make yourself look like the best prospect for an inheritance?

Was this family not only greedy, but dangerously so, and did Big Brother fear that he might put a target on his back? If only one in the room could inherit from the father, then this could become an elimination game where the strongest candidate got knocked out first.

"My father called me a waste of space. Large space," the big man said. He tried to soften things with a smile. "I was the only child for seven years, yet never felt like the favourite in all that time. And that situation didn't change when the others came along. My father, the big time producer, only had time for his other productions, and for this place he poured money into, Egypt. Or the ancient relics of it. I became rebellious, crossed him constantly, dropped out of college, spent my allowance on drink, disappointed him in every way. So no, my chances of being the sole heir to my father's estate are a lot slimmer than I am."

Big Brother was damning his own prospects.

"Then what if I suggested you killed your father?" Daniel put it to him.

"Are you? I'd say he was dying anyway. Why kill my father? I didn't know before he died that he was thinking of choosing only one to inherit. None of us did."

True enough.

The eldest of the two close-knit sisters put down her glass.

"Okay, I think I speak for my sister here too –"

"You usually do," Computer Man said.

" – when I say that our father had contempt for his daughters. He thought of us as spinsters, literally, homebody material more interested in craft than careers. He made us feel we were failures. We could never remember anything about ancient history, he said. But he was the typical patriarchal rich man who probably never expected anything of us anyway."

"And wasn't disappointed," Computer Man muttered into his glass.

"Did you or your sister, or both of you, get rid of your father?" Daniel said.

"Knock our father on the head and heave him overboard? We're more subtle than that, in spite of what our father thought of us."

"Thank you. So far you've all made convincing cases for being left out of the Will."

"I've got something to say." Bad Cop spoke up. "I've never heard anything like this in all my years on the force. You call this an investigative interview? Is this how you're going to dig up the perpetrator? You just can't do community interviews."

"Yet here we are," Daniel said. "So what about you and your brother?"

"Look, he had a grudge against me all his life."

"And you had a grudge against him for being rich," a Sister piped up.

"A rich guy who saw me as police hack," Uncle Bryan said.

"You mean as a cop turned bad who got thrown out of the force for using excessive violence?" the other sister added.

Bad Cop glared at the two sisters as if he was on the verge of throwing an Edwardian glass at them.

"I can top that," Computer Man said. "I disappointed my father most of all. I ended up in prison for computer fraud. I hacked people's accounts, including my father's."

Maybe they had tongues marked with the feather of truth, too, Daniel thought.

They were all being brutally honest in discounting themselves.

"This dream cruise has turned out to be a game after all. A deadly game," Kate said as she lay beside him in their antique brass bed in their cabin while the *Belle Epoque* lay moored overnight at Asyut.

"What are you thinking?"

"I'm thinking of the old man lying dead on board with us, like one of those ancient Egyptian mummies in their wrappings as they made their ritual *post mortem* voyage by river to the holy city of Abydos."

"That's depressing."

"What's even more depressing is the fact that I'm not making much progress. Maybe archaeologists and detectives are in sister professions, but you can unearth a lot more with a trowel."

"You were clever about the paddles."

"But I'm still missing something."

"Like the identity of the murderer, maybe? Look, I know they're not a loving or loveable family, but honestly, do you really think one of them did it?"

"I honestly do."

"Okay, then tell me the truth, who's your chief suspect?"

"I honestly don't know. Maybe I'm out of my depth. I'm steering this investigation in the wrong direction, into the shallows, and I've hit the bottom of the river where I'm stuck, high and dry."

"That's a lot of riverboat metaphors."

"It's the truth about how I feel."

"Maybe this new side of you is not such a bad thing, Daniel. This new streak of honesty. I like hearing about a man's feelings. I feel you're opening up and we're getting closer."

"We could get even closer," he suggested.

Suggestively.

She chuckled and tickled him.

What was it about death, sex and eternity?

It was an eight-hour sail to their next stop of Sohag.

Eight hours of uninterrupted cruising up the Nile.

And pondering.

Maybe the constant movement of travel would help move his investigation forward.

That morning Daniel was morosely deliberating the situation over a breakfast of 'Eggs Benedict served with mushrooms sautéed in butter and basil', when Legal Suit dropped in to join them at their table, a glass of orange juice in hand.

"How was your exploratory dig for information last night?" he said.

"Fruitful, I trust." Was he expecting a progress report?

Daniel couldn't lie.

"It turned out to be a quiz without answers," he said. "It didn't sound to me as any of them should expect to inherit from their father. Surely, as his confidant, you know something."

"I am still in a privileged position and I take my duty seriously. Therefore I am not at liberty to divulge anything."

A man of great probity and one with a deep keel. Hyman Robbins was not swayed by events. This was not a man driven by the moral laws of the Ten Commandments:

Thou shalt not kill thy rich and neglectful father

Thou shalt not covet thy greedy siblings share of the inheritance.

Thou salt not steal by hacking thy father's account.

Thou shalt honor thy quirky father...

Instead, Hyman Robbins was governed by the law of contract, and he would observe the letter of the law to the end.

Daniel left Kate on the upper deck to read her book on Egyptian mythology. He revisited his thinking place.

The splashing paddle wheel and the rural landscape of eternal Egypt only alarmed him today as if answers were passing him by, along with time.

Only one more stop overnight in Sohag and then they would be at Abydos.

He wondered if Calder Hall, stiffening like a mummy in the boat's cool room, sensed that he was drawing closer to his beloved archaeological site of Abydos, the *post-mortem* destination of pilgrims past?

Should they go ashore and make a site visit?

Why not?

Daniel longed to see Abydos again for numerous reasons.

First, his own curiosity about Abydos had never been satisfied. And it seemed like an act of respect to his employer to carry on his pilgrimage. Kate would enjoy the beautiful artwork of Seti's temple and the family of the dead man needed a break. They'd been pacing around the boat looking as restless as caged animals, all the while keeping a wary look over their shoulders.

The *Belle Epoque* was changing from a luxurious cruise boat into an ancient Egyptian funerary barque, Daniel thought.

A stretch of the legs might help everyone.

He attended the morning tea and coffee with Kate, but the family feared another quizzing. The place was empty.

Only Legal Suit and Mayet came.

The rest of the morning and lunch went by in a blur of contemplation, as did the afternoon break where Daniel was the only one to turn up this time. Kate had taken a nap in the cabin.

Dusk was settling on the Nile when he paid another private visit to Calder's suite. Nothing had been touched, by his request.

The sharp nose of the jackal-dog walking stick challenged him as he entered and closed the cabin door.

"Do you know something, Jack?"

He picked up the mobility aid and gave the jackal-dog's head a swing like a seven iron at a par three golf hole. Then he put it back against a chair and wandered around the suite.

Something said by somebody at the quiz night was stirring in his brain.

The golden computer, still lying open at the antique desk, caught his eye.

The computer.

Was that it?

Ideas collected other ideas like jars in a *felaheen's* water wheel.

Daniel delayed the serving of dinner.

The family, gathered in the Dining Saloon, muttered.

He went out in front.

"According to our cruise itinerary, tonight was supposed to be a Black and White Party. Everybody was meant to dress up in formal black and white. We haven't, but let's not waste the theme. I am going to give you some truth tonight. In black and white. I will tell you who killed Calder Hall."

That stopped the grumbling over the late dinner.

He let the impact set in.

"I recall the eldest son's remark last night. He said: "Why kill my father? I didn't know before he died that he was thinking of choosing only one to inherit. None of us did."

The family turned stares on Big Brother.

"You think I did it?" he said.

"You raised an interesting point," Daniel went on. "Why kill a dying man? Or more significantly, why kill Calder Hall *before* you heard he planned to limit the inheritance to one beneficiary? None of you knew, you said. But was that in fact true?

It was as if someone knew the process and status of Calder's private deliberations on his Will and wanted to head off something before Calder could put a drastic change into effect. How did they know?"

He glanced in the direction of Computer Man.

"I recall the computer loving member of your family confessing that he disappointed his father most of all. He ended up in prison for computer fraud. He hacked people's accounts, including his father's. Then I recalled how wedded he was to his laptop at the start of our cruise. He was back in the hacking business and his locked up computer will show the evidence. He hacked his father's computer in search of clues about how the old man was thinking. Another giveaway? Calder's computer. His apps and programs had begun to crash. It's one of the warning signs that a computer has been hacked. That's why Calder asked his son to look at his computer in his suite and his son agreed, brazenly taking advantage of the opportunity to kill his father with a now missing bottle of port, before tossing him overboard. He was running out of time and he had to act because his chances of inheriting in the will looked hopeless. That accounts for his sudden burst of magnanimity, which I happened to overhear, his suggestion that you draw up an agreement that whichever family member was named as the sole heir at the end of the cruise, they would waive their right and agree to share the inheritance equally among all. It was the only way to cover all bases, but he had to stop his father in his tracks. The proof of his hacking ways will be there for an expert to prove when this cruise is over.

Computer Man didn't argue.

He scraped back his chair and knocked it over, sending it crashing to the Dining Saloon floor.

He bolted for the doors.

Daniel was already springing after him.

"How far do you think you can get?"

The son disappeared out of the door as the Dining Saloon broke into uproar.

Computer Man fled down a companionway to a flight of steps with a curved wooden railing and disappeared. He was heading for the floodlit promenade deck.

Daniel pounded after him.

Taking two steps at a time, he emerged on the deck to hear the drum of running footsteps.

Computer man was sprinting down the promenade deck.

It wasn't going to get him far.

Computer Man glanced back over his shoulder, saw Daniel closing and clambered up the deck rail.

He reached the top, paused, then sprang out into the darkness and hit the Nile with a sharp splash, then vanished.

Legal Suit and Bad Cop came running up.

"He's jumped ship," Daniel said. "Going on the run. He won't find it easy getting out of the country with his passport still on board."

"You let him get away?" Bad Cop said, appalled. "Stop him!"

"You want me to dive in and search the inky black waters of the Nile? It's your nephew, so please, go ahead."

"You would never have made a policeman, Buddy!"

The death dogs of Abydos

CHAPTER 8

Post mortem pilgrimage

They travelled in two vehicles to the desert plain of Abydos, embayed in the distance by mountain cliffs - the burial ground of Egypt's earliest royalty and the site of temples built by later pharaohs Seti and Rameses the Great.

The mummified dead from all over Egypt came on *post mortem* journeys of pilgrimage to this burial ground of the god Osiris - and also of Khentiamentiu and Wepwawet, if Daniel was right.

Daniel thought of Calder Hall's fondness for this place and pictured the old man's *ka*-spirit shuffling along, jackal-dog walking stick in hand, haunting the exquisitely decorated seven sanctuaries and two hypostyle halls of the temple of Seti as the visitors passed through them, trailing the murmuring voice of a local Egyptian tour guide. The temple of Rameses lay nearby, reduced to a dilapidated state with mostly a few courses of stone remaining. Daniel's gaze went further afield to the ruins of a mud brick temple in the northwest, an old kingdom temple dedicated to Khentiamentiu.

The sight of it, and the conjuring up of the name Khentiamentiu, brought back Daniel's old hunger to explore that he so often subdued these days.

"Do you mind if I leave you and the lawyer to keep an eye on the fractious family for a while?" he whispered to Kate. "The guide will take you on to the Osirieon next, a mysterious sunken temple built out of megaliths with water and an island down below. They used to think of it as another tomb of Osiris,. I'm going to slip away and ask our driver to take me on a spin across the plain to look around."

"Enjoy," she said. "I'm loving this tour and just stretching my legs."

Their Land Cruiser followed the direction of the ancient processional *wadi* that led to the tombs of the first Dynasty pharaohs, including that of King Djer, the symbolic tomb of Osiris.

The plain also held Ibis and dog cemeteries in honour of the death dogs of Abydos.

"Where are you, Khentiamentiu?'" Daniel murmured to himself.

They bounded in the four-wheel drive vehicle over the desert terrain while he studied it through the windscreen and passenger window.

Rubber-on-the-ground archaeology, he thought, as they crossed the ancient plain of the afterlife.

The man-god Khentiamentiu, represented by a jack-dog, bore a title.

"Lord of the Westerners.' Westerners, referring not to a cardinal point, but to the direction of the setting sun, the land of the dead.

"Maybe we'll go closer to the mountain cliffs," he suggested.

The driver changed course.

The decision almost catapulted them into the land of the dead, when a rip of gunfire smacked into the side of their vehicle.

The driver scowled in his rear view mirror.

"Bad. Maybe looter gang."

"What do they want with us?"

"Not me. Their bullets are all on your side. Do you have something they want?"

"Only my skin, apparently."

"I saw men follow your group into the temple from the car park," the driver now informed him.

"Okay, maybe it's time to cut this excursion short. Can you get us away from these lunatics and back to the temple?"

"Hold tight, Sir."

The driver swung in a sharp circle and hit the accelerator, surging towards their pursuers. A risky move because as they approached on a collision course, an attacker leaned out of a window and took another shot that blew away Daniel's side mirror.

"I said get us *away* from them."

But the driver had a plan.

He spun the Land Cruiser at the last moment, just as they hit a soft bank of sand. The swerving vehicle threw a broadside of sand into the windscreen of the oncoming attackers, blinding them.

The man-made sandstorm prevented them from seeing a hidden outcrop of rock. They hit it on the driver's side and it threw the vehicle over.

Looking back, Daniel saw it spinning on its back like a stranded tortoise.

The sand of Abydos could be a weapon as well as hide secrets.

Who were they?

Calder Hall's deadly murder mystery game was over.

Why try to kill him?

He rejoined the group as they were returning to the car park outside Abydos temple.

"No dramas in the temple?" he said.

"None, but you look a bit shaken about," Kate said. "No dramas on your desert drive?"

He wanted to say no, but the truth took over his tongue.

"Oh, you know, a mad car chase and then gunfire from a band of antiquities looters, that sort of thing."

"Sure, Daniel."

In the afternoon they sailed on to Nag Hammadi, where the *Belle Epoque* moored for the night.

The mood on board had lifted a little after the Abydos excursion and they brightened even more over cocktails at sundown, followed by bottles of wine over dinner. The sisters closed ranks with Big Brother and shared a table with him at dinner. Daniel and Kate sat at a table nearby and the lawyer dined alone at another. Uncle Bryan also preferred his own company.

The dinner and the night that followed were uneventful.

But not the morning.

Legal Suit marched in with the sober air of a lawyer serving a legal document, the young Egyptian camera girl following in his footsteps.

"There's been another death overnight."

Big Brother.

No signs of anything suspicious.

"He died in his sleep, it appears."

"The Sisters?" Daniel said.

"Distraught," Legal Suit said.

He didn't need to ask about ex-cop Uncle Bryan.

He'd be exploding.

Even if he was the guilty party. Maybe more so.

But he remained an unlikely candidate in Daniel's view.

The Sisters would be his first choice.

But why would they take such a spectacular risk?

Only... if they were absolutely certain that their involvement would never be proved.

Daniel met the ship's doctor in the boat's surgery.

The young filmmaker Mayet was there too, recording it all, camera in hand.

If this continues, the old man could have a ring of subsidiary burials, Daniel thought grimly.

The doctor drew the sheet off the bulking form on the bed.

"A big man, it could have been a heart attack," he said.

"Not poisoning?"

The doctor dropped his voice to a confidential murmur.

"By poisoning I take it you don't mean food poisoning. There is no sign of say arsenic poisoning, which leaves bluish discolouration in the mouth area. More likely it was a brain aneurysm, a silent killer that can strike anyone at any time.

A remarkable convenient occurrence, Daniel thought.

Time for a chat with the sisters.

He visited them in their cabin. They let him in and retreated to a couch where they resumed their knitting with neurotic intensity.

Maybe they planned to yarn bomb the boat.

Mayet recorded the discussion.

"When did you last see your big brother?" he said.

Click, click, click...

The sound of deathwatch beetles.

"We had an after-dinner drink in the bar and then separated. We came back to our cabin."

"We know what it must look like –"

" – and we know what you must be thinking –"

" – that you are the last ones with any motive to harm your brother."

Now he was finishing their sentences. "Your Uncle Bryan has never been in the running."

"Maybe."

"But we didn't do anything."

Maybe, like Isis and Nephthys, they were spinning a shroud for their brother's body.

Daniel inspected Big Brother's cabin. The bed was still rumpled, everything left as it was.

No sign of violence.

His shoulders slumped.

What would a detective do now? Go over the details again. Repeat an examination of the facts.

What would an archaeologist do?

Dig new exploratory trenches? In which direction? Try some ground penetrating radar to look below the surface?

Belle Epoque continued on the next leg of the cruise and arrived at Qena at mid morning.

A tour to the temple of Dendera was in the offing and it was a temptation, but out of the question after recent events. And yet the temple of Dendera was one of Daniel's favourites, dedicated to the goddess Hathor.

He had always admired the double-headed columns inside the temple with capitals showing twin images of a cow-eared woman.

The Female Soul With Two Faces.

Like the Sisterhood, he thought.

Stony.

But right now he desperately needed to see below the surface.

Below the surface?

Time to repeat an investigation of the evidence.

Uncle Bryan interrupted him on his way. The ex-cop came boiling up the stairs and grabbed Daniel by his shirt. He shoved Daniel against a curved wooden railing, tilting him off his feet.

'Excessive use of force' was probably a valid charge against him after all, Daniel thought, and there was excessive strength in the grizzled man's grip. Daniel wondered if he needed to kick himself free with a well-aimed knee.

"Listen, archaeology man, you're screwing up and I've had enough. Another death and you haven't even interviewed me."

Daniel tried to keep calm.

"You sound disappointed. You angling to be guilty?"

"I could be guilty of hurting you right now with one push."

"Don't."

 "What happened to my nephew Leo?"

"Enquiries are proceeding –"

"– don't give me that police statement bullshit."

' – and progress is expected soon."

Uncle Bryan relaxed his grip and Daniel sank back to the step.

"That better be true."

Legal Suit and Mayet, the voyage filmmaker, joined him at a second meeting with the sisters in their cabin.

"We told you everything," the sisters said.

Stone Hathor, Female Soul with Two Faces

"Everything? A classic case of pulling the wool over my eyes. I underestimated you two. Your late Big Brother warned me that you have clever fingers, but you're also manipulative. I imagined you weren't even listening to my lectures as you sat there with your balls of yarn and flying knitting needles. But you listened all too closely. You knew you weren't going to win a massive inheritance by knitting."

"Or listening to lectures on ancient history."

"Ancient history was all our father cared about. Not us."

"Do you know what the boat's doctor found when he examined your brother in his surgery? Nothing. Not a mark. Like the 'unblemished beast sacrifices' of animals. Or those murdered servants and subjects of early pharaohs that I talked about in my lecture, their practices of so-called 'retainer sacrifices' and 'subsidiary burials'. I conjectured about how the victims might have been killed. Strangulation? Poison? Or maybe by means of a sharp instrument penetrating the brain, say from under a raised eyelid, where it left no mutilation, not even blood. Especially if somebody used a sharp instrument for the murder - like a fine knitting needle."

The sisters gave up knitting at precisely the same moment.

'Now only their foreheads are knitting in displeased frowns,' he thought.

"Here's how it happened," he said. "You encouraged your brother to get rolling drunk at dinner and afterwards, probably helping him back to his cabin, where he passed out on his bed. Then you took one of your finest knitting needles, flipped an eyelid up and goodbye Big Brother and your rival for a fortune. The trace of a puncture to the brain was almost invisible, but after my suspicions, and a second examination by the doctor using a magnifying glass, he found it. I'm sure a proper autopsy will confirm it. Quite subtle, Ladies."

"And our father thought we were stupid –"

"– and never remembered anything about ancient history."

"You will remain confined to your cabin, behind a locked door until the end of the cruise at Aswan," Legal Suit said.

"We're prisoners?"

"You'll have your meals and refreshments brought to you."

"And you'll have all the time in the world to knit," Daniel said.

"Especially after your trial."

VIDEOCAM CAPTURES DANIEL LEAVING THE CABIN. **(Young female voice, off camera):**

"You must be pleased with that stroke of inspiration. No detective would have solved that. It took specialized historical knowledge."

"Thank you, but I'm left with the awful thought that my lecture gave the sisters their idea. They had no interest in ancient history, their father said. So I excited their interest and fed them a piece of arcane historical conjecture that got the eldest brother killed. And I thought knitting was a gentle pastime!
It must have taken nerve on their part, and greed, to go through with it."

Well played, Daniel," Kate said later. "The sisters were doing it for themselves,"

"Yes. And so well co-ordinated they could have knitted together with one set of needles, like two hands playing chopsticks on a piano."

"But did you ever notice what they were knitting?"

"No."

"Scarves. Yards and yards of them," she said.

"Like mummy windings. Those two always made me think of Isis and Nephthys, weaving what were called the 'tresses of Nephthys' for the body of the dead Osiris. That only leaves Uncle Bad Cop now. But I'm sure he doesn't stand a chance of scoring the inheritance."

"Then I wonder what happens now? Who inherits?"

"Probably archaeology. Some university institution."

"Then why play games?" she said.

Ironic, coming from Kate, he thought.

"You mean he should have just given it to archaeology straight away and saved all this violence? Calder was a successful movie producer, remember. They're no strangers to violence. And he hated his family as much as they hated him. He also wanted one last bit show."

"Sad."

"Murder, I'm discovering, is a sad business. Sadder than archaeology, digging up the past..."

Karnak Temple

CHAPTER 9

"Tell us the truth!"

While Daniel appreciated the funerary beliefs of the ancient Egyptians, a funerary barque was not his idea of a cruise.

Now there were two bodies on board.

As well as two killers in detention.

The *Belle Epoque* churned onwards to Luxor, amid growing cruise boat traffic that clotted the artery of the Nile. They berthed at the busy tourist hub, with the backdrop of the Winter Palace Hotel facade and the columns of Luxor Temple dominating the town.

Luxor - once famed as *'Thebes of a Thousand Gates'*.

Now a thousand entry gates, Daniel reflected. Ticketed entryways to great temples like Karnak and Luxor, Medinet Habu, Deir el Bahari, tombs in the Valleys of the Kings, Valley of the Queens and nobles, the Western Valley, the fine Luxor Museum and more...

He needed this escape.

Daniel, Kate, Mayet and the lawyer took a break from the boat to make the tour. Uncle Bryan stayed on board.

First stop was a trip by vehicle across a Nile bridge to explore the Valley of the Kings and Hatshepsut's temple. It was Kate's first visit and the carved and painted underworlds of the tombs beneath the valley, deep and glowing, enthralled her with every step.

For Daniel, the tombs this time were like a sense of failure closing in, especially the small dimensions of Tutankhamun's tomb.

Luxor and particularly Karnak temple, with its acres of stone and crushingly huge hypostyle columns added a weight to his spirit. Could he have done more to anticipate disasters?

"My client, Mr Hall is a quirky man, as he readily admits," Legal Suit had said. "He likes putting people in situations."

'He's certainly put me in one,' Daniel thought.

It should all be over, but there was something unfinished about this Murder on the Nile Mystery Cruise.

He needed time alone to think.

He left Kate and Legal Suit with the Egyptian guide to complete their tour of Karnak's adjoining open-air museum and strolled out to the car park.

The temple was a lot emptier than he remembered on past visits and the car park was the same, with fewer coaches, minibuses and cars in evidence.

Maybe he'd take a rest in the air-conditioned vehicle and wait for the others to come.

The driver would be waiting, probably smoking a cigarette outside.

Daniel circled a blue coach. It had curtained off windows.

They weren't curtains to keep out the sun.

Three men jumped him and before he could struggle hauled him on board the bus.

It wasn't over.

The three Egyptians, in western clothes, worked him over inside the
cigarette smoke fug of the bus and the fourth one left the driver's
seat to help.
Blows rained on Daniel like the rotating paddles of the riverboat that
had clubbed the body of Calder Hall.
He was groggy and his head spinning when they flung him down
into a front seat.
"Search him."

Fingers dug into pockets, hard hands frisked him.

"Is that what you wanted to do to me at Abydos, when you tried to
shoot me? Hoping you'd find something on me? What?"
"Nothing on him," the searcher said.
Then the interrogation began.
"You tell us the truth. How long do you know rich man Calder
Hall?"
"I only met him only once before."
That got him a slap.
"The truth."
"Once."
"Another slap across the cheek.
"How long?"

"Only once before and when he hired me..."

Another slap. The truth could be painful. What did they want him to say? Lie and say that he was a lifelong confidant? They'd prefer a lie evidently, but he couldn't get his tongue to say it.

"He knew a secret about Abydos, but he was dying," the Egyptian inquisitor said. "Dying with his secret. Then he calls on you. Why?"

"I don't know why. I wish he hadn't."

A ripping backhand across the other cheek now.

Daniel's head rang.

"Why did he hire you? What did he say when he first hired you? What did you talk about?"

"Dogs, walking sticks, Abydos..."

"Aha, Abydos. What did the rich man know about Abydos?"

More truth was probably going to get Daniel another slap.

"He liked the place. We both had a special interest in it."

"And your special interest?"

"Just a wild theory about lost tombs still to be found in Abydos."

"Did he know about such a tomb? Did he ask you to join him in finding it? What is in this tomb?"

"Maybe the treasures of Khufu?"

The Khufa theory had always been a stretch for Daniel, a hypothetical teaser, and sounded much more so now.

"Khufu?" The interrogator slapped Daniel harder. "You think we are stupid? That is the biggest lie of all. The Great Pyramid was Khufu's tomb."

"Yes, but..."

Crack.

This blow went across the head.

He couldn't help letting out a loud groan.

"Tell us the truth!"

Daniel blinked up at them blearily.

"Okay, your coach door had just opened and two armed tourist police are coming in here."

"Lies!" But the interrogator turned to look and so did the others.

It was not some lame trick to divert them so that he could turn the tables and fight his way out.

Two policemen, rifles pointing, were there.

Somebody must have seen the attack and reported it.

"Step out of the bus. All of you!"

The doctor aboard the *Belle Epoque* checked out Daniel on his return.

He'd survive, with a few painkillers to ease the aches and pains.

"So you really were shot and chased back at Abydos," Kate said.

"I told you the truth."

"You made it sound like a lie."

"It just sounded unbelievable. Like that attack at Karnak."

"What is happening, Daniel? Something is going on besides this Nile murder nightmare."

"Calder Hall liked putting people in challenging situations. I just don't know which one he's put me in now."

That night the sisters committed joint suicide in their cabin.

Tablet overdoses, the doctor said.

Why hadn't Daniel anticipated the danger?

Uncle Bryan wondered too.

"We've had two murders, one escape, and two suicides on your watch, Buddy. That adds up to one big balls-up!"

Hardly a successful investigation, Daniel supposed, even though he did pick the killers.

"Well, don't take things too hard," he soothed the ex-detective.

"Hey, you're the last man standing. But at least you're innocent, well not of everything. You've never been a suspect here. And never a prospect to inherit. In fact, I've been wondering why you're here at all. And I think I've worked it out. Your brother liked putting people in spots. He knew a detective would make things tough for me and provide an entertaining contrast to an Egyptologist at work and that's the only reason he invited you along."

The last two stops of Edfu and Kom Ombo went by in a blur of painful memories and puzzlement for Daniel.

Everybody stayed on board.

Then they arrived at Aswan, a rural town in Egypt's far south.

They berthed opposite caramel cliffs with sweeping stairs that climbed to reach the Tombs of the Nobles.

The end of the Nile murder mystery cruise felt like an anticlimax.

Aswan tombs

But it wasn't quite over. There was still the remaining part of the Will to address, which Legal Suit insisted on doing in a corner of the public lounge aboard the *Belle Epoque,* joined by the official recorder Mayet, behind her camera, and Uncle Bryan seething in his chair.

Daniel was surprised to see the lawyer rest the old man's walking stick against a coffee table.

The stick rocked and the golden jackal-dog shook his head.

"What else is there to learn?" Daniel said. "I suppose Calder Hall's fortune is going to Big Archaeology - some overseas university with missions in Egypt?"

"No. One of my deceased client's relatives survived the cruise."

Daniel blinked in surprise.

"You mean Uncle Bryan, here?"

"No, I'm afraid. Sorry," he said to the ex-policeman who grunted.

"Why am I not surprised?"

"Then the young ship jumper, Computer Guy? He's been found?"

"No. He will be found and arrested, be assured, but not him, either. Someone else will inherit the fortune. Someone who remained hidden throughout the cruise."

That took a moment to sink in.

"A stowaway?" Daniel said.

"Not exactly. She is watching us right now - from behind that camera."

"Mayet?"

Daniel swung to the camera.

All he could see of her head was the front of the camera and her beret poking out on top.

"I can now disclose that producer Calder Hall's young filmmaker protégé is in fact his unrecognized daughter to an Egyptian woman twenty five years ago. But now the daughter is recognized, and handsomely so!"

Mayet, the unseen one, hidden behind the camera all the time. The silent observer, like an invisible narrator of a drama, her recorded images running like a stream, or river of consciousness through a journey of over half a thousand miles.

Calder Hall had set her secretly among her undeserving siblings for a telling, side-by-side comparison. It suddenly made the father's threat of only ONE beneficiary a little more understandable.

Mayet was the sole heir.

Calder was launching the young Egyptian into a career of big filmmaking with a fortune at her disposal.

Daniel had never seen that coming.

He too had looked for some tiny redeeming feature in the legitimate family members. If one of them had a glimmer of virtue in spite of their criminality, it had been Computer Man. During the family's discussion after the bombshell announcement, he had made the suggestion that whoever inherited should forgo their rights and share equally with the others. He had also shared some of his ill-gotten gains from hacking in the past with his ungrateful sisters.

"Did any of the other family members come close?" Daniel asked the lawyer.

"I am not at liberty to speak about that. But now that the cruise is over, you will of course be paid the full balance for your services."

"Thank you. Well there it is. I suppose we'll now call in the Egyptian authorities to try to clean up this mess."

"Yes. But first there was a small bequest for you, a gift, a memorial of Mr Hall, if you like. He wanted you to have this." He picked up the golden-headed walking stick and handed it to Daniel.

"He's giving me the stick? Hello, Jack," Daniel said to the jackal-dog, clasping the stick in his hand to address the canine head.

"My former client also left this message for you."

The lawyer read out a note:

"Daniel, here is a gift for you. The Opener of Ways.

Here's hoping he can help you open the ways to your dream discovery.

I like giving people challenges... and I'm leaving you with one."

"Please thank the Estate of Calder Hall for me," Daniel said. "Maybe with my luck I'll break a leg next and really need this guy." He turned to the camera. "You can come out now, Mayet. Time for the hidden filmmaker to take a bow. Congratulations on your sensational inheritance!"

The camera trembled.

Mayet came out now, smiling, dampness on her cheeks.

"Lucky Mayet," Kate said afterwards in their cabin. "Funny if she had been the murderer all along, while hiding behind the camera."

"Please Kate, no more. I'm over murder mystery games."

"But it's possible, you know. Think about it. She would have had access to the old man's computer too. She told us the old man watched updates of her footage at the end of each day. How would that happen? She'd download footage to his laptop for him to view at his leisure. Maybe he trusted her and turned his back and she saw something on his computer. Thought she had a chance of inheriting something, but the old man was dithering in his deliberations and so she had to stop him making a change."

"Oh, God," he said.

Had he been wrong all along?

"But why would Computer Guy jump off the boat in such a guilty way?" he said. "If Mayet was the guilty one?"

"Maybe they were both guilty. Maybe they had discovered each other's secret prying into the old man's computer diary notes and decided to act together."

"Oh God," he said again.

"The look on your face. I'm only teasing. I don't believe Mayet is like that at all. She is a lovely Egyptian girl. Trust my instincts."

Kate was always going to be playful and games were going continue he thought.

"Oh, good," he said, but it made him a little fearful about how close he might have come to the brink of disaster as an archaeologist detective.

"And yet..." she said.

"Stop it."

They packed to leave the boat.

Legal Suit had booked them into Aswan's Old Cataract Hotel overlooking the rock-strewn Nile, the last stop on their itinerary, where they would stay as the official investigations proceeded.

CHAPTER 10

Opener of Ways

Daniel and Kate were relaxing on the Old Cataract balcony that overlooked the Nile. Down below, tilting sails of feluccas cut the blue water like white diamonds as they glided past.

The Egyptian police had swarmed over the *Belle Epoque*, statements had been taken, followed by polite, but tireless questioning. The missing son had been picked up by authorities and would be duly charged.

"This grand hotel, perched on a cliff above the Nile, is where Agatha Christie wrote her detective novel *Death on the Nile*," he told Kate over a beer on the hotel balcony. "I wonder what she would have made of our little murder mystery game?"

"Not enough bodies or red herrings for her."

"Quite enough."

"That stick suits you, you know Daniel," she said, eyeing the jackal-dog walking stick resting on the table edge between them. "Gives you an Edwardian air. Gentlemen sported sticks in those days, didn't they?"

"Jack and I are just bonding. I think he's hoping we're going to provide his new 'forever home'."

"Forever? We?"

He nodded, picked up the jackal-dog's head stick and made the canine nod too. She laughed and patted its head.

The Opener of Ways.

There seemed to have been a loaded significance in Calder Hall's last message to him, the thought kept teasing him.

The old man had left him with the *Opener of Ways*.

"Here is a gift for you. The Opener of Ways. Here's hoping he can help you open the ways to your dream discovery. I like giving people challenges... and I'm leaving you with this one."

"Hang on," he said.

"Changed your mind already?"

"Maybe I need to do a little more digging, with Jack."

"Jack? What do you mean?"

Daniel grasped the head of the walking stick and gave it a twist.

"Why are you strangling him?"

The jackal-dog resisted. Daniel's hand trembled with the force he applied, then, like a jammed tap handle suddenly giving way, the dog twisted his head.

"There."

Now the golden head spun as Daniel unscrewed the walking stick's handle.

"What are you looking for? One of those old fashioned swords in a cane?"

"No. But something equally pointed."

She sat up.

"What?"

The head came off to reveal an empty tube.

He peered down it. Not quite empty. A rolled up cylinder of paper lay coiled inside.

He shook it out, put the jackal-head and stick on the table and unfurled the paper.

"It's some kind of map?" she said, excited.

"Correct."

He squinted at the drawing. It showed an embayed plain with mountains, temples, cemeteries marked on the surface.

One of these, a dog cemetery, had been ringed in red ink with a single word beside it.

'Khentiamentiu!'

The *eureka!* name.

But not a lost tomb, it was only a dog cemetery.

Unless... there was a hidden tomb below it in the depths of Abydos sand.

Was that why it had remained hidden from archaeology? Not even ground penetrating radar had seen it because it was disguised by the structures of the dog cemetery above it?

Dead dogs, concealing the death dog Lord of the Westerners.

"What is it, Daniel?"

"The key. Calder Hall has given it to me. And the biggest challenge of all. To spend my future trying to convince Big Egyptology to listen."

THE VIDEO FINDS EGYPTOLOGIST DANIEL CANE
LOOKING PENSIVE, BUT RESOLVED NOW.
HIS SHOULDERS RELAX.

"So now I have the truth.

**And the truth is that Calder Hall's game continues with a
different challenge of detection - an archaeological one. How did
he come by the knowledge he has passed on to me? He had many
contacts in legitimate Egyptology and it would be surprising if
he didn't also have a few on the shady side too.**

**It could be that this story is still the beginning and the issue of
Calder Hall's legacy to his family was merely a violent backdrop
to a more astounding legacy - a secret that he knew I would
never give up on.**

**Modern Egypt has suffered instability, a revolution, wholesale
looting, a crisis of tourism worsened by a pandemic that has
spurred illicit digging and trafficking. Maybe somebody came
across something and owed Calder a favour, so they shared a
secret discovery with him. A secret others would desperately
want to know. I may never find out the answer.**

**It remains to be seen if, after bringing archaeology to mystery
murder detection, I can now bring detective skills to archaeology
and uncover the truth about Khentiamentiu."**

Daniel checked the surface of his tongue in a bathroom mirror of the
Old Aswan Hotel.

Had the mark faded a little? It was still discernible.

'What if it's there for good?' he thought.

Ancient Egyptians believed that magic was about unseen, hidden connectedness between things, words, ideas, dreams, truth, reality, symbols...

Maybe he was stuck with something.

A marked man.

He'd played a role of investigating crimes with the mark of Maat upon him, finding truth, weighing the guilt and innocence of others in the balance.

Was he fated go on playing the role of an archaeologist detective?

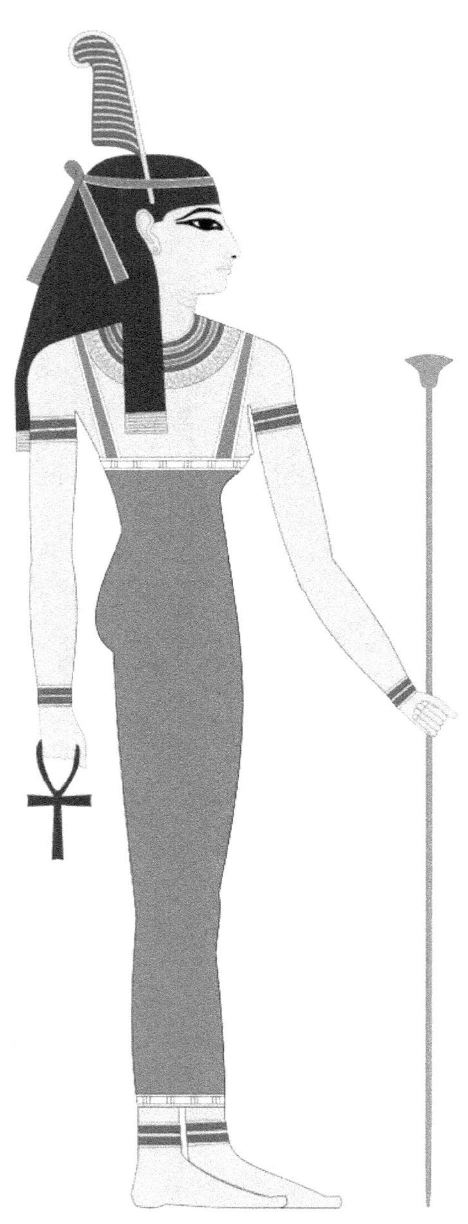

Maat, goddess of Truth and Justice. Wikipedia

About Roy Lester Pond

Roy Lester Pond is a prolific author of ancient Egypt-inspired fiction. His depth of knowledge comes from a lifetime spent studying ancient Egypt and Egyptian archaeology. He has been to Egypt on numerous research trips. Roy is fascinated by the mystery of ancient Egypt and its potency and relevance for today's world. 'The Smiting Texts' was his first archaeological thriller, followed by a series featuring renegade Egyptologist Anson Hunter, as well as other stand-alone adventures. Roy spent much of his life in Africa and now lives in Australia. Roy Tweets regularly about Egypt and adventure fiction writing under the Twittername "Egyptsnippets" and writes a blog 'Ancient Egypt

Fiction&Facts'.

124

Mystery of Egypt Collection by Roy Lester Pond

The Egyptian adventure series featuring Anson Hunter, alternative Egyptologist, battling dangers from the ancient past:-

ROY LESTER POND
THE SMITING TEXTS
HATHOR'S HOLOCAUST
ROY LESTER POND
THE IBIS APOCALYPSE
A BOATLOAD OF EGYPTOLOGISTS, A NIGHT OF DIVINE JUDGEMENT
THE NIGHT OF ANUBIS CRUISE
ROY LESTER POND
ROY LESTER POND
THE FORBIDDEN GLYPHS
EGYPT EYES
ANSON HUNTER ARCHAEOLOGY THRILLER
Roy Lester Pond
ROY LESTER POND
THE GOD DIG
ARTEFACT
ROY LESTER POND
AN ANSON HUNTER THRILLER
ALEXANDER'S LOST EGYPTIAN ORACLE
ROY LESTER POND

New

THE ANSON HUNTER series or archaeological mystery adventures

Hidden dangers from Egypt's past, modern-day conspiracies that take their impetus from Egypt's ancient mysteries.

 The Smiting Texts, Hathor's Holocaust, The Ibis Apocalypse, Hidden Egypt - The Night of Anubis, Egypt Eyes, The Forbidden

The first three Anson Hunter novels in the 9-novel series – in one Kindle edition. Fiction's favourite independent, renegade Egyptologist. The Smiting Texts, Hathor's Holocaust, The Ibis Apocalypse

*****5-star fiction Amazon/Goodreads

THE EGYPTIAN MYTHOLOGY MURDERS

A mummy named Isis is taken to a hospital for a non-invasive imaging scan... so begins a mystery and a string of deaths.

An ancient cycle unfolds in modern day London - and a search for eternal love.

Can Jennefer, a young trainee museum curator and Jon, a police antiquities unit detective, stop the killings in time before a terrible culmination of events?

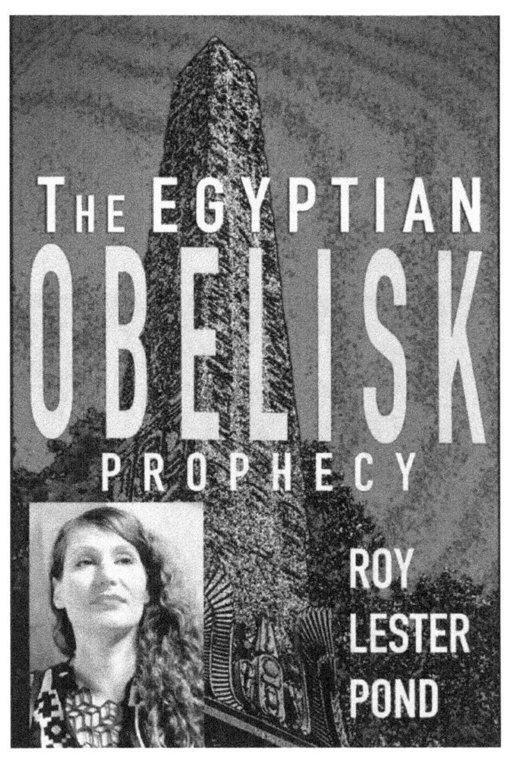

The EGYPTIAN OBELISK Prophecy

What was the Obelisk Prophecy?

The exciting fiction sequel to 'The Egyptian Mythology Murders'.

Detectives and Egyptologists are in sister professions. Now the unusual team of Jennefer, an Egyptologist museum curator, and Jon, an arts and antiquities policeman, is back together in 'The Obelisk Prophecy". Egyptian obelisks are potent symbols that pierce the skies around the world. London, New York, The Vatican...

But now one obelisk represents the clue to a world-threatening mystery.

Working against secret enemies the team must race to find and penetrate the riddle of the one obelisk on earth that holds the key to salvation.

THE EGYPTIAN CROCODILE QUEEN

When a new blockbuster ancient Egyptian exhibition arrives, mysterious events and a string of killings soon follow.

The investigative team of Jennefer, a curator, and Jon a police antiquities detective, must track down the shocking truth in a hidden underworld beneath the city - and discover a shocking secret from ancient Egypt, linked to a modern day conspiracy that takes its impetus from the ancient past.

In the unnerving footsteps of THE EGYPTIAN MYTHOLOGY MURDERS and THE OBELISK PROPHECY.

THE EGYPTIAN MUMMY WRAP MURDERS

4th book in the enthralling 'Egyptian Mythology Murders' mystery series.

The spell of a vintage reel of film shot at a dig site in Egypt in the early 1900s.

A crumbling mummy in the private museum collection of a Grand English Castle today.

A mummy called Nephthys, the same name as the Egyptian goddess who wove the cloth mummy wrappings of Osiris, called the 'Tresses of Nephthys'.

A series of graphic murders...

Is the terrifying onslaught building to an event that will affect the world?

And what is the secret of the eerie, nonverbal young daughter of the Earl?

Investigative team of Jennefer, a British Museum Egyptologist Curator, and her partner Jon, an Antiques Unit Detective, have just hours to stop a countdown to catastrophe.

TRILOGY. THE EGYPTIAN MYTHOLOGY MURDERS: 3 TITLES IN ONE EDITION

Ancient Egypt resurrected...

3 Egyptian mythology-driven mystery thrillers set in the modern day, but with a twist of the ancient unknown.

A unique investigative team of Jennefer, a museum curator, and Jon a London antiquities detective - two very different people who work in 'kindred professions'...

The X-Files meets 'The Mummy'...

- THE EGYPTIAN MYTHOLOGY MURDERS

A mummy named Isis is taken to a hospital for a non-invasive imaging scan... so begins a mystery and a string of deaths.

An ancient cycle unfolds in modern day London - and a search for eternal love.

Can Jennefer, a young trainee museum curator and Jon, a police antiquities unit detective, stop the killings in time before a terrible culmination of events?

- OBELISK One Egyptian obelisk is the key to saving civilization

- THE CROCODILE QUEEN MYSYERY An Egypt exhibition, a series of mythological murders

ARCHAEOLOGIST DETECTIVE SERIES

THE EGYPTOLOGIST DETECTIVE SERIES.

Meet Daniel Cane, archaeologist and sometimes cruise Egyptologist, who finds himself digging for murder clues in Egypt instead of for buried artefacts.

MURDER ON THE NILE MYSTERY CRUISE

MURDER IN NUBIA

ARCHAEOLOGY OF MURDER

THE SHABTI DOLL MURDERS

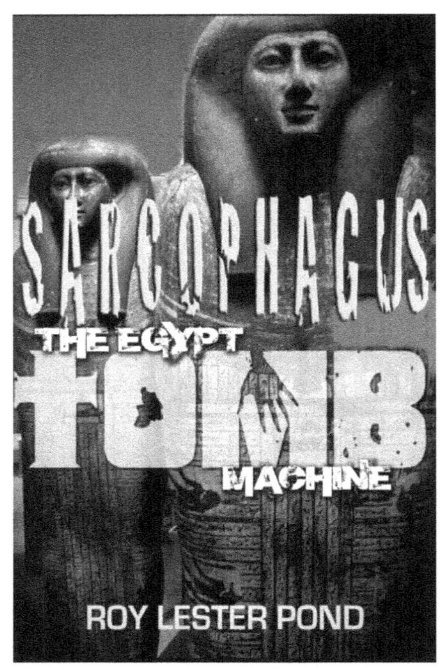

THE SARCOPHAGUS

Adventure, mystery, fantasy. An archaeologist with a
bow shoots an arrow into adventure...
In the modern age, Ryder an archaeologist in Egypt
discovers a mysterious empty sarcophagus in a tomb.
Then his Egyptologist partner Janet goes missing.
He vows to go after her, even if it means journeying
across the boundaries of reason and existence. Ahead of
Ryder and his Ridgeback dog lies a pre-dynastic realm
of myth: the mysterious Mistress of the Bow and Ruler
of Arrows, the evil Lord Set, legions of animal-headed

creatures, the venerable bird-man, the child Horus. And key to it all is the quest for the magical amulets of power. A life-and-death struggle is on at the edge of time. And the universe watches - and waits.

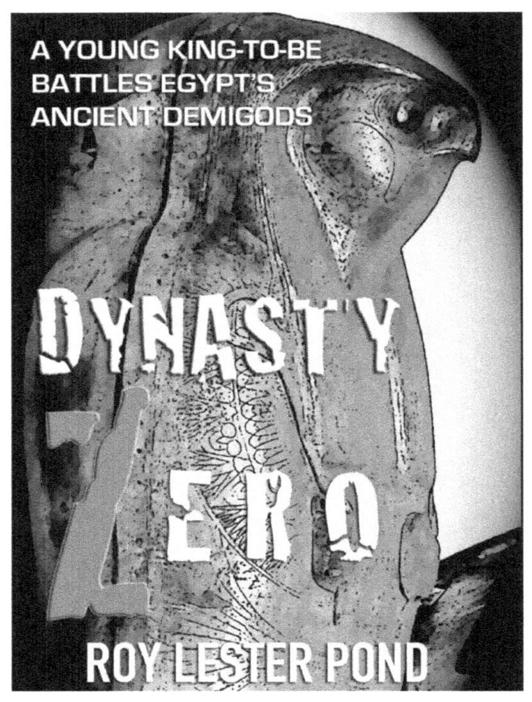

DYNASTY Zero

A primordial clash of humans, gods and demon demigods.

A young demigod boy Nemes, a future unifier of pharaonic Egypt, also known to history as Narmer, lived on the fault line between deity and humanity. It was a time of the gods and demigods, when the throne of the god Horus shook and the weak hands of men stretched out to catch the crown and seize the scepter of Egypt. The demon demigods did not stand by, but seized the moment to strike.

I, THE MUMMY

Preserved in the 'Tresses of Nephthys' - the sacred wrappings of linen woven by the goddess Nephthys and tied with the'magic of knotted cords' of Isis, an immortal soldier hero rises to fight Egypt's greatest enemy - the ruthless Hyksos invaders and occupiers...

Action adventure thriller.

Awakened after a thousand years in a tomb sanctuary filled with weapons...

The Ancient Defender arises to fight against a ruthless oppressor.

The Hyksos have seized Egypt at a time of weakness following the Middle Kingdom, overpowering all with their superior technology of chariots, hardened bronze weapons and compound bows.

And they are now plundering Egypt for its forbidden secrets of power.

Can ancient history's most unlikely hero stop them and resurrect a divided land before the Hyksos can gain Egypt's most powerful and dangerous secret of all?

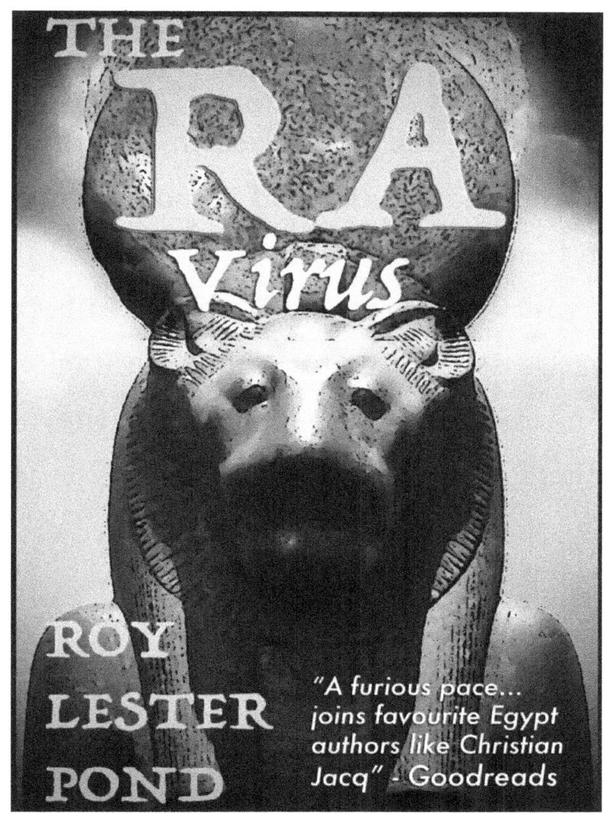

THE RA VIRUS

Is a vanished archaeology team member trapped in Egypt's ancient past during an age of terror – and sending warning messages to today?

'WARNING! ANCIENT GLOBAL THREAT…' the graffiti message appears in a newly found Egyptian tomb, along with a modern biohazard symbol.

What mysterious plague has hit the population of Egypt in the reign of Pharaoh Amenhotep III and his young co-regent, the sun-struck Akhenaten? Why is it seen as a judgement by the angry sun god Ra? An eleventh plague of Egypt?

Lucas, a physician and World Health Organisation expert on pandemics, must find its source and the antidote in time to save the ancient past and the future. Especially when his lover, Egyptologist Giulietta in the modern age, is exposed to the deadly contagion. Can he warn her in time and save her - and can they ever hope to be reunited?

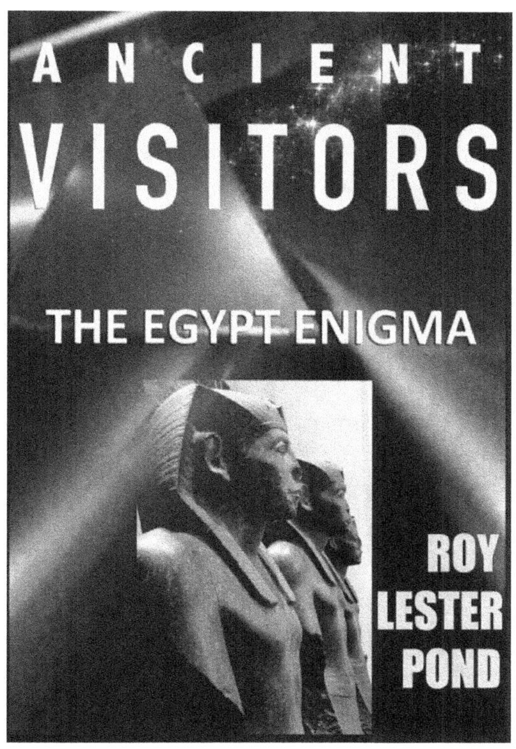

'Ancient VISITORS The Egypt Enigma'

In the field of ancient civilizations, 'visitors' meant one thing to Egyptologist Rebecca Landers.

The controversial theory about the enigma of Egypt and its advanced technological achievements.

Then came the surprising evidence... and a threat to the world.

Suddenly she and her team were called on to span two worlds on a dangerous archaeological quest like no other.

Only they had the power to save history and the future.

EGYPT EXTRACTION

TIME JUMP ERA: 3 A.D.

MISSION: Save the Jesus child, a refugee in Egypt, journeying with escaped family.

THREAT: modern day Islamic Time-Terrorists and ancient assassins of Judean King Herod...

Time-travel terrorists... drones... attackers with assault weapons racing through the Nile's papyrus reeds... their target a boy king.

At stake, the future of civilization.

Standing in their way, two young time jumpers, Salome and Callen of the Anti Time-Terrorist Strike Force. They must stop a catastrophe that could affect billions of lives and the belief systems of the world. Sci-fi, ancient history and time-travel novella with a startling twist and revelation.

Plus AVATAR EGYPT

An ancient Egyptian simulator game turns deadly real.

EGYPT TRAP

Keep an eye on a mysteriously obsessed young wife

visiting the archaeology sites of Egypt? How hard could

that be?

A damaged ex-detective is hired to shadow a girl with

painted eyes on a trip to Egypt...

Is she leading him step by step into a murder

conspiracy and the mystery of a lost ancient Egyptian queen?

Dan Loader reluctantly accepts the job. A damaged, former-detective from a police Art and Antiques unit, he is already traumatised by an ordeal at the hands of antiquity traffickers. Yet he desperately needs something to help him hold his life together and following the girl looks like a soft surveillance task, more so as he becomes increasingly drawn to her. Rich, independent Kate Barnsdale is a beautiful, haunting young woman surrounded by an unmistakeable aura of ancient Egypt. Her obsession with a lost, mythic Queen from Egypt's 6th Dynasty seems to be taking over her life.

When she insists on travelling to Egypt alone to follow her mysterious urgings, her husband hires Dan to shadow her secretly and watch over her.

But is Dan being drawn step by step into a murder conspiracy that involves the secret of a mythic queen from Egypt's ancient past?

Crime and suspense with the mystery twist of ancient Egypt.

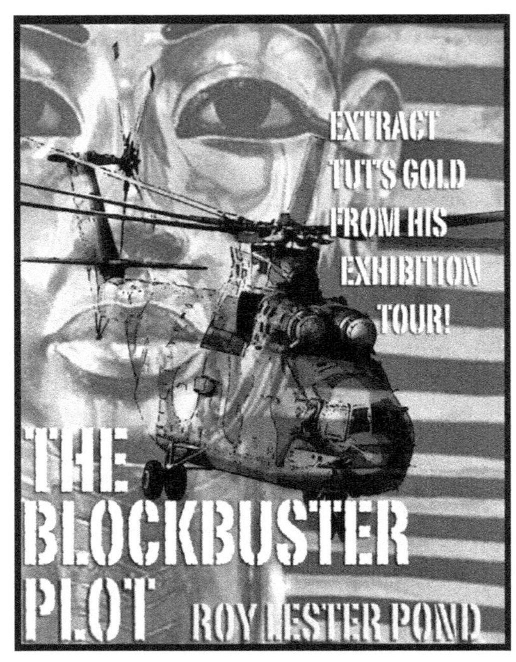

THE BLOCKBUSTER PLOT

The Boy King's Gold... a Blockbuster USA Tour... a dazzling display of criminal daring.

It was an outrageous plot:- Extract Tutankhamun's priceless gold on its blockbuster tour of the USA. *But who is the enigmatic mastermind behind the disappearing act and why have they done it?*

Will they demand a pharaoh's ransom for its return? And what will become of a pair of US hostages, a museum Egyptologist and a female National Geographic feature writer traveling with the treasures?

A golden target, the most famous treasures in the world... *gone...* the fabulous golden artefacts of

Tutankhamun, about to appear in the USA in the biggest blockbuster exhibition since the world wide pandemic, have been stolen.

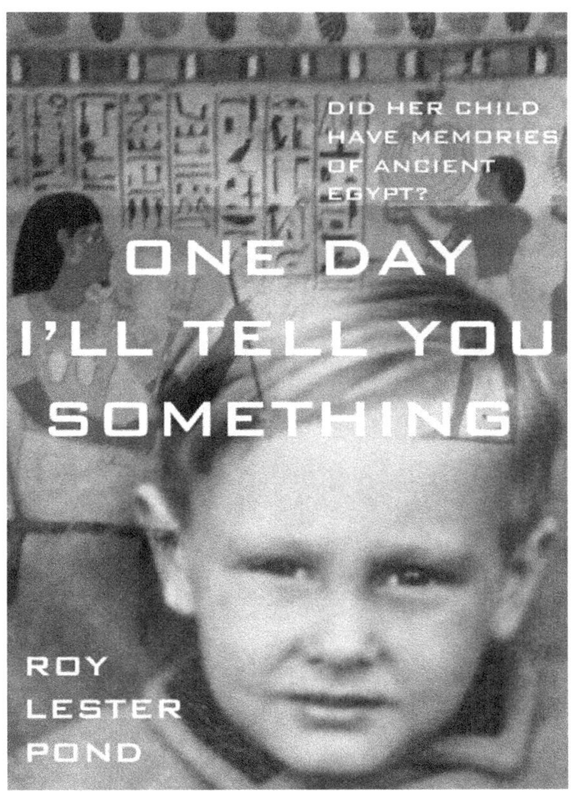

ONE DAY I'LL TELL YOU SOMETHING

A child obsessed with the ancient past, a young mother who discovers adventure...“

I remember Egypt," Cooper said gravely. “Long, long ago.”

Her little boy was gorgeous, she thought, but his imagined past life could be a bit hard to take. Especially at 8.30 in the morning, when she was busy having a this-life crisis, running late for work and her eight-year old was about to miss his school bus.Then young single-mother Catherine meets a past life researcher and also a mysterious Egyptologist Simon Priestly and she and Cooper are off to Egypt on an extraordinary quest to follow a young boy's dreams... or are they actual memories of the ancient past?

What will they find and what will Catherine find as she warms to the impressive British Egyptologist as they uncover a shattering secret from Egypt's past? Disturbing and intriguing adventure fiction with a twist of the unknown.

THE VIRTUAL EGYPT GAME - a group of players, including a female Egyptologist, play a deadly virtual reality running game inside a mysterious simulator of ancient Egypt's dangerous underworld. Then they start dying, for real.

THE GHOST OF THE BRITISH MUSEUM

There is a certain statue in the Sculpture Gallery of the British Museum of the son of Rameses The Great, Egypt's most illustrious pharaoh.

The statue has an eerie attraction even today.

In the 1900s a London group known as The Society of Inner Light regularly conferred with the exhibit in the Egyptian Sculpture Gallery, convinced that it was a medium for metaphysical activity and emanated unseen forces.

She was an American historical writer visiting the British Museum's Egyptian Sculpture Gallery to research a new book.

He was a legendary and enigmatic prince from ancient Egypt who desperately needed to undo a terrible mistake.

Was the strange young man's sudden materialization before Madeline just 'cosplay', or the result of an attraction between two souls across time?

Would they share a mysterious quest on a journey through Egypt, and much more?

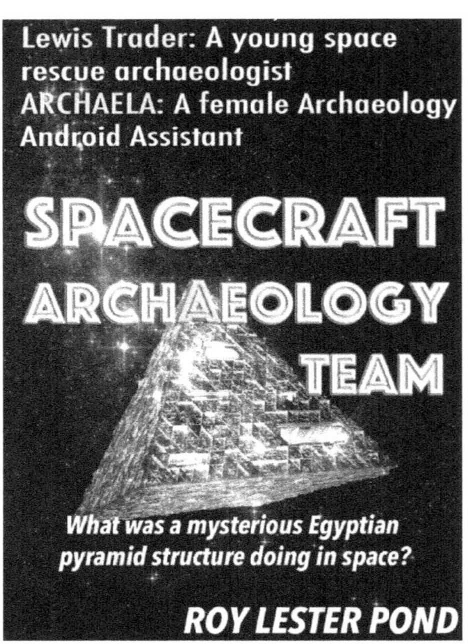

SPACECRAFT ARCHAEOLOGY Team

Lewis Trader: A young space rescue archaeologist
ARCHAELA: A female Archaeology
Android Assistant

Was it a space mirage? A lost pyramid structure
abandoned in space...
In the future, a space archaeologist Lewis Trader and
his female archaeological android ARCHAELA make a
discovery.
A glowing ancient Egyptian-style pyramid floating
among the stars.
They begin a climb up guarded ramps inside the

structure amid rising levels of tension – their progress challenged by mysterious, lethal guardian sphinxes... leading to a startling revelation.

THE PRINCESS WHO LOST HER SCROLL OF THE
DEAD

2 Egypt Fantasy Titles in One.
1. The Princess Who Lost Her Scroll of the Dead
Her priceless Book of the Dead is swapped for a blank
one by a greedy royal scribe... How can Nefera find her
way through the dangerous gateways and guardians of
the Egyptian underworld without her magical spells -
her passport to the world beyond?
And who is the boy tomb robber Ipy, sharing her

journey? Is he alive, or dead?

2.

MUSEUM GHOSTS

Karoy and his companions - a squad of Egyptian wooden soldiers created to protect a tomb owner - arise when the Lady Tiy is stolen from the museum. Can they rescue her from the outside world?